BILLIONAIRE WITH BENEFITS

MAKE HER MINE-BOOK 2

ALEXIS WINTER

A NOVEL

By
Alexis Winter

I KNEW HE WAS MY BOSS

I knew he was my brother's best friend.
I knew he was a bad idea...
But when he's 6'4" of solid muscle
And a filthy mouth that has you screaming his name...
What's a girl to do?
We laid out the ground rules:
1. No feelings
2. No commitments
3. Nobody finds out
In my defense, I tried to walk away.
But the moment I tasted his lips,
My fate was sealed,
And my panties melted.
It was all just delicious fun,
Until it wasn't.
Now it's not only my heart on the line,
But his future at the company.
I can't let him destroy his life for me.
Instead, I'll break my own heart and walk away.
After all, we never promised each other forever.

PROLOGUE

MADDIE

I STIR awake as the sheet drags across my bare skin. I blink against the sun that's streaming in through the cracked curtain and sigh as the feel of a large, warm hand travels up my thigh.

"Good morning, beautiful," he murmurs against my throat, followed by a soft nibble.

A shiver runs through my body as his tongue dances softly against my neck. I groan softly as my back arches off the bed, needing more from him. He senses my anticipation as he trails his fingertips from my knee up my inner thigh, dancing briefly across my clit, causing my hips to jut up further.

"Mmmm, does my naughty girl like that?" He teases me again, letting his fingertips stay a little longer this time, dragging them across my clit a few more times ever so lightly.

"I want—" the words trail off as my eyes close, and he sucks my earlobe into his mouth. His breath comes out in soft, warm puffs against my cheek as his finger slips between my folds.

"What do you want? I want to hear the words." I reach my hand down to force his fingers harder against me, but he grabs my wrist before I can make contact.

"Tsk, tsk" he clicks while fastening both of my wrists above my head. He places his hand beneath my chin and forces me to look at him in the eyes.

"What do you want, Madeline? I told you I want to hear it. Whatever you need or desire." The last part is a whisper as he leans down and plants a soft kiss on each of my very pert nipples. I groan as he bites them after the kiss.

"I need to cum—I want...I want you to make me cum." The words tumble from my mouth in a rush as he smiles against my breast.

"How?" My mind is a blur; I feel like I'm about to burst.

"Your tongue, hands. Lick me." The words continue to come out in a staccato pattern. Finally, he releases my hands as he moves down my body to settle between my thighs. He inhales as he runs his nose up my center before flicking his tongue across my clit. I can't contain the loud moan that escapes my throat as I fist the sheets in my hands.

He grips my thighs with each hand, his fingertips digging into my flesh as he devours me with voracity. His slow licks transform into deliberate flicks of his tongue peppered between deep passionate kisses against my most sensitive and intimate parts.

No man has ever made my body feel this way. No man has ever had this kind of power and control over my body, causing it to explode with ecstasy over and over. Even when my brain is telling me I can't possibly handle more, my body betrays me and surrenders to his every desire.

I can't hold back my climax any longer. Sweat beads on my forehead as my body stiffens and arches. Hips bucking against his face as he crooks his finger, I explode in pleasure. My vision blurs as the orgasm tears through my body, leaving me in a satisfied, limp puddle of limbs on the bed.

He crawls up my body and settles between my thighs, pressing his lips against mine as his tongue explores my own. I can taste my release on his mouth as his rigid cock presses at my opening, and my thighs fall open to welcome him.

His eyes lock on mine as his hips begin a rocking motion. He intertwines his fingers with my own, once again pinning them to the bed and using the leverage to thrust himself into me even further. The moment is deep and intimate. Emotions swirl through my head as I try to drown them out and live in the moment. This thing between us started as purely physical; we promised each other no labels and no commitments. I thought I knew what I wanted. I thought I could keep feelings out of it, but now, I can only hope to survive the fallout when he walks away.

MADDIE

"Pick up the phone," I say as the line rings for what has to be the twentieth time.

"Hello?" Jazz, my best friend—fiancée to my brother and expectant mother of his baby— answers around a giggle.

"Finally! What the hell were you doing?" I ask, clearly annoyed.

"Nothing. What's up?"

"I'm getting ready for my first boxing class, and you said weeks ago you'd go with me."

"To be fair, that was before I found out I was pregnant. Damon doesn't think it's a smart decision."

"Ugh, what does my stupid brother know? Plus, it's not like we're going to actually be fighting. We'll hit the bag a few times. And it wouldn't have killed you to let me know before right now."

"I'm sorry, Mads, but I don't think so." I can hear the uneasiness in her voice.

"Come on, Jazz. Please come with me. Just this once, or until I meet some people and get comfortable."

"I don't know. I mean, Damon and I kind of had plans for tonight."

I hear her softly giggle and whisper, "Quit it, I'm on the phone."

"Seriously? You had plans with ME first! Jazz, did you forget you're my best friend first and his fiancée second? Since you guys have been hooking up, we don't ever see one another anymore. Come on. It's only for one hour, and then you can go home and do whatever you guys do with your nights." I silently gag at the end of that sentence.

"Okay, okay. You're right. I'm sorry." She lets out a sigh of defeat. "I'll be over in an hour."

"Thank you," I say, hanging up the phone. I hate having to play the *you were my best friend before his fiancée* card, but hey, a girl's gotta do what a girl's gotta do.

I drop the phone onto the couch and get up to change my clothes. I pull on a pair of black leggings and yank off my shirt to replace it with a lime-green sports bra. I check myself over in the mirror as I pull my hair up into a messy ponytail, then slide on my shoes. I do a few chores around the house, and just as I'm grabbing my jacket, phone, and keys, Jazz is walking in the door.

She lets out a deep breath and drops her purse on the table. "This is going to be a lot harder once Damon and I move out of the city, you know?"

I nod my head. "I know. All those nights we snuck out of the 'burbs to come to the city, and now you're moving back there voluntarily."

She offers a sad smile. "I know. But it's perfect if you think about it. I mean, how many people get to raise their kids in the same place they grew up? And with their childhood crush, no less?"

"It is kind of perfect." I stick my tongue out at her for having such a fairytale life.

She laughs. "I don't know what you expect me to do at this boxing class in my current condition." She motions toward her stomach that's still flat.

"You can do anything I'm going to do. It's the first class, so it's not like we're going to be fighting one another."

"Good, because I promised Damon that I wouldn't even put on gloves." She laughs.

"He thinks you're going to a boxing class to not box?" I ask, pulling my jacket on.

"He thinks I'm going for moral support."

"Why does he think that?" I ask, holding the door open to let her walk out first so I can lock it behind us.

"Because that's what I told him?"

We both laugh as we walk down the hall toward the main exit.

Twenty minutes later, we're at the gym, boxing gloves in place. I promise Jazz I won't tell my brother. The big room has punching bags hanging from the rafters and a ring in the far corner. The instructor tells us to warm up by jumping rope and trying out the bags. At first, we take turns holding the bag for our partner to hit. After a good twenty minutes of this, the instructor gets our attention again and has us sit down to watch two trained members fight as he walks us through what they're doing and why they're doing it.

Jazz and I sit ringside on the floor. The instructor is a middle-aged man with cropped graying hair and arms like pythons. A large vein runs down the center of his bicep. If I had to guess, I'd say he's the owner, and these are the fighters he's trained. Two more men join him in the ring.

I bump Jazz's elbow with mine. "Whoa! That guy is sexy as FUCK," I whisper so only she hears.

She nods her head and purses her lips together. "I guess. He's got nothing on Damon though."

I scoff and roll my eyes. "You two make me sick," I say, watching the man that's caught my eye.

He has dark hair that's shaved short, nearly to his scalp, and five o'clock shadow that does little to mask his chiseled jawline. Every time he jabs, his entire body flexes, and let me tell you, there's not an ounce of fat on his delicious physique. Every single muscle looks hard as a rock, like he's been hand carved out of granite by the gods. His chin is defined, with a small dimple in the center.

Suddenly, his emerald green eyes cut to me, and I feel like a kid caught with her hand caught in the cookie jar. He gives me a quick smirk, and I lick my lips as I feel my face grow red before looking away.

They fight for several minutes, and if you ask me, it isn't nearly long enough. Then, the three men move out of the ring and onto the floor.

"All of you, go back to your bags and use the information we just gave you to improve. I want to see you strict on form. Plant that back leg and lean into the punches you throw. We'll all be walking around the room, giving you pointers," the older man says.

Jazz and I stand up and move back to our punching bag. She holds the bag and I step in front of it. Curling my hands into tight fists inside my gloves, I hit the bag over and over. I actually forget where I am, paying no mind to the people around me or the sexy man that could be watching me. I'm focusing all my energy on that bag and the power behind my punch.

"You have pretty good form. Is this your first time?" the sexy guy asks, stepping next to Jazz, facing me.

I let my arms fall to my sides as I nod my head, unable to speak. I don't know if it's because I'm breathless from the relentless punching or if it's because I'm at a loss for words given how much sexier he is up close.

He has his arms crossed over his sculpted chest, causing his biceps to bulge as he looks me up and down. "Can I give you some pointers?"

"Of course," I agree, trying to sound nonchalant. In reality, I'm about to melt into a puddle on the spot.

"Take your position," he orders.

I bring my fists back up.

He walks a circle around me.

"Spread your feet," he says, gently pushing them further apart with his foot.

I do as he says.

"Straighten your back." He places one hand flat on my spine, causing me to suck in a breath from the electric current that cuts through me. He steps to my side and places the other hand on my stomach. "Tighten your abs. Can you feel that? The difference in how you were standing and how you're standing now. You're taller, tighter. All your muscles are under your control. Keep that core engaged; don't let your spine hunch."

I nod, now focusing more on how his hands are touching me rather than listening to what he's saying.

"Now, jab!"

I extend my arm and hit the bag. It makes a thumping sound that fills my ears.

"Good. Keep your wrist straight," he tells me. "Again!"

I extend my arm again, this time focusing on keeping my wrist straight. The blow is much more solid than the previous ones.

"Better. Now, when you swing, put your whole body into it. Again!"

I swing with all my might while keeping my wrist straight. The strike is solid and powerful.

"There," he says, letting his hands drop. "Much better."

"Thanks," I say a little too breathy for my liking.

He looks at Jazz. "You need some tips?"

She shakes her head. "Nope. I'm only here for support."

He lets out a deep chuckle. "Alright." He looks back at me, but he doesn't just look at me: his eyes roam up me until our they meet mine, like a lion staring at an antelope he's about to devour. "Keep going. I'll check back with you later." Without another word, he walks away to help the next person.

For the rest of the class, I watch him out of the corner of my eye, checking to see if he helps another person the way he helped me. He doesn't touch them at all. The most he does is walk by with a nod, sometimes offering a quick comment. I'm not sure if I should be creeped out by that knowledge or accept that maybe my form was just that shitty.

When the class is dismissed, Jazz and I stand at the counter, removing our gloves.

"Hey, what happened to the guy you were dating? Travis?" Jazz asks, arching an eyebrow.

I roll my eyes. "Travis was fun." I shrug. "He was like a toy, but you know, all toys get old after a while. So, I donated him for the next girl to enjoy." I smile.

Jazz shakes her head. "One of these days, the love bug will bite you."

I laugh. "I don't know about the love bug, but I'd definitely take a hit from that sexy boxer."

"Is that right?" he asks, stepping up behind me.

My face immediately heats up and I bite my lower lip as I turn around to face him. *Shit!*

He offers me a grin as his eyes travel up my body again. "I'm here most nights. If you want a private lesson, you know where to find me." He shoots me a wink and walks away.

When he's far enough away from me, a long breath I didn't realize I was holding escapes my mouth and my shoulders fall.

"Really? You couldn't tell me he was behind me? Mouth, meet foot."

Jazz laughs. "I thought it'd be funnier this way. Not to mention, now you have a reason to come back."

I grab my jacket and pull it on. "I already had a reason to come back; now I have a reason to completely avoid this place."

"What? Why would you do that? I thought you wanted to take a hit from that boxer?" she teases.

I bump her arm with my elbow. "Because I'm completely embarrassed!"

"Oh, you'll be fine. I've seen you recover from much worse. But on another note, I'm meeting up with Damon for dinner. Want to join? We're going to your favorite pizza place."

"I don't want to be your third wheel," I complain.

She opens the door and walks out onto the sidewalk. "Seriously, it's always been the three of us. Nothing changed, Mads."

"Nothing changed? Jazz you're carrying his baby and you guys are in a relationship. Now you have all the little inside jokes and communicate with stupid looks like you and I always did." I know I'm sulking, but I'm still not over the moon that I was pushed out of the group. "Whatever, I'll go. But I'm ordering my own breadsticks."

She laughs. "Deal."

Jazz and I walk into the pizza place a little while later and Damon is already at a table waiting. When he sees us, he stands and pulls Jazz in for a hug and a quick kiss. I slide into the booth and pick up a menu.

"How was the class?" he asks.

"Well, your sister got hit on by a hot boxer," Jazz says, wrapping her hands around Damon's arm.

"That's gross," Damon mumbles, picking up his water and taking a sip.

"I didn't get hit on. I got invited to a private lesson." I smile, just hearing myself saying the words.

"That's worse. Who is this guy?" Damon looks between the two of us, brows pulled together and eyes bouncing from her to me.

"I didn't catch his name, but he has sweaty muscles for days, dark hair, a face I could mount, and bright green eyes. Like, his eyes were green-green. Not your dull, boring green."

Damon holds up his hands and waves them back and forth violently. "I NEVER want to hear those words again, Maddie. Jesus!"

"I think your eyes are gorgeous, babe," Jazz says, squeezing his arm.

Damon smirks as he turns to admire her.

When they start kissing, I can't help but roll my eyes and sigh loudly. I'm still not over the disgust of watching my brother suck my best friend's face.

"We seriously need to find Maddie someone to settle down with," Jazz says, running the tips of her fingers up and down Damon's forearm.

"You guys are killing me. I mean, can't we just have dinner like we used to? You know, you two throwing insults at one another, making me laugh? Now it's like a god damn porno every time we hang out."

"Oh, I have my first doctor's appointment tomorrow. We get to find out how far along I am and see our little baby," she gushes, ignoring my comments.

"I thought you were six weeks along?" I ask.

"Well, that's what I'm guessing, but I have no real way of knowing because we were just doing it all the time," she laughs. This is usually the talk I like, but knowing my brother is involved makes me want to barf.

"Ew, all right. I've had enough. I'm going to grab a hot and ready pizza on my way home. You two, enjoy your night," I say, scooting out of the bench.

"No, Mads, please stay. We don't hang out much anymore," Jazz says, trying to stand up to stop me, but she's on the inside of the booth and Damon isn't moving.

"You know, I'm really tired, and I'm just going to crash. But thanks for the invite and for going with me." I'm already walking backward toward the door, so they can't stop me.

The moment I step out into the cool night air, I feel like I can finally breathe. I suck in a big breath, hold it a second, and let it all out. I can feel the annoyance and stress leave my body at the same time. I hope Jazz and Damon don't think that I'm not happy for them, because I am. I'm celebrating that they got together, but I'm also mourning the loss of my best friend. She's no longer just my best friend; now she's his fiancée, and soon, she'll be a mom.

Jazz just got her dream job too. Her life is going places, and I'm still stuck in the mailroom, waiting for my desired position to open up. When I started a year ago, I was told it would only be a couple of weeks before I could move into data configuration, but here I am, still stuck sorting mail.

I don't have my dream job. I don't have a special person to share things with. I'm not about to have a baby—thank god. And, I no longer have a best friend that's always down to hang out. What do I have?

I have a large pizza to myself. I smile as I look down at the warm box and take in a big whiff of the gooey cheese.

When I get home, I kick off my shoes but don't bother to change. I drop all my takeout on the coffee table and flip on the tv. I flop onto the couch and pull the blanket around myself. As I search for something to watch, I move all the food up onto the sofa, so I don't have to reach for it. I look around my lonely, quiet apartment and wish I had someone to share this with. I never understood why people got into serious relationships until I saw Jazz and Damon. They're literally never alone. They work together and then come home to each other. They always have someone to talk to, someone to eat with, and someone to hold them when they feel lonely. Maybe I should put myself out there and make it clear I want a relationship instead of random hookups and flings.

I shake my head. What the fuck am I thinking? I like being single. I like getting dressed up and looking hot. I like the chase. I like a no-strings-attached fling. I like having complete control over the TV, and I like for things to be where I left them. I'm obviously way too tired if I'm even considering giving all this up.

I push all thoughts away as I dig into my food and watch reality TV all alone, with nobody to complain.

2

BENNET

"Who was that girl you were practically eye-fucking over there?" Phillip asks, taking off his gloves and tossing them into his bag. I shrug. "I don't know who she is. And I wasn't eye-fucking her. What are you, a seventh-grader?" I tease, pulling my shirt on.

He laughs. "You know what I mean. You were obviously flirting. I haven't seen you help someone with their technique like that in a long time. Since Bethany, I think."

I think back to Bethany. We had hit it off immediately when she came in for some boxing lessons. Sparks flew and we had the fling of a lifetime. But, like most girls, she wanted more, and I wasn't willing to give anything else. Our relationship consisted of nothing but flirting, fucking, and leaving. It lasted a good three months before it ended, and I've been on the lookout for someone to have fun with since. I'm not a complete piece of shit; I let the women know out the gate I'm not looking for anything more than a good time.

I wave my hand in the air. "I doubt this girl ever walks back in here again. She seemed kind of…"

"Hot? Really into you? Almost jumped you when you were pawing at her?" he inserts.

"Shy," I finish.

"She didn't shy away when you grabbed ahold of her."

I laugh. "That was the test. But did you see how red her face got when I caught her talking about me? I invited her for a private lesson, but I doubt I ever see her again." I grab my bag and pull it up over my shoulder. "I don't have time to get involved with a woman who doesn't know how to handle me, if ya know what I mean. I'll see ya tomorrow night."

He waves as I walk out of the locker room.

I toss my bag into the passenger seat of my convertible Mercedes-Benz AMG and hop behind the wheel. Twisting the key, the engine roars to life. I hit the gas a couple of times to rev up the engine before shifting into gear and taking off, causing the tires to squeal off the damp concrete.

I drive through the city, thinking about making a stop at my favorite club, but I end up deciding that I'm too tired to play the usual games tonight. You know: find the girl, woo the girl, take the girl home. I don't feel like having to ask her to leave in the morning. Plus, it's a Sunday night. I have to be at the office bright and early in the morning. I don't need to give my dad any more excuses to try to take the company back.

I pull into the drive, my sensor opening the gate. I pull the car into the garage and make my way into the house.

"Good evening, Mr. Windsor," Quinn, my house manager, says, standing at attention. She's normally gone by this time of night. I'm tempted to ask her why she's still here so late but don't bother.

"Evening," I respond, grabbing a beer out of the fridge. I turn and look at her. She's young, and her blonde hair is pulled up high on her head. She has long tan legs and big tits I've noticed more than just a few times and a pink pouty mouth. She looks just like any girl I'd pick up at the club. Only problem is, she's my employee, and if I sleep with her tonight, I'll end up having to fire her soon after. That's how it always goes, I've learned my lesson after hiring, fucking, and firing three house managers in a six-month period.

I shake the bad idea from my head. "I'm heading up to bed. Have a good night."

"You too, Mr. Windsor."

God, her voice is so sweet. She's like a siren, singing a song that only I can hear. I get to the swinging door and turn around, giving her one last look, trying to talk myself into asking her to come up to my room. She looks at me with her big blue eyes. Her pouty lips part and her full chest rises.

I open my mouth, about to say *to hell with it*, but I snap it shut and leave the room before I can change my mind. The whole way up the stairs, I'm fighting with myself. *Just ask her to come up.* But if I do that, I'll end up looking for another manager by next week.

Quinn was hired by my mother when I mentioned needing some assistance around the house. I refused to tell her why I let the last one go, but it was because I got trashed and invited her to my room. After a week of trying to get her to understand that it was just a bodily need and poor decision made under the influence of alcohol she still insisted we were 'meant to be.' So, I had to fire her. She would get all pissy when I'd bring other girls home. I even found her naked in my bed one night. I like women and the comfort they bring, but I also like having my own life and space. I don't want someone else's life intertwined with mine.

I let myself into my room and walk straight through to the bathroom. Turning on the hot water, I strip down to nothing and step beneath the flow. The heat eases the sore muscles in my back, and it calms all the thoughts inside of me. I'm no longer thinking about women, drinking, or sex. Finally, my head is quiet, and I can relax.

I hit the button that turns the shower into a steam room, and I have a seat on the bench while drinking my beer. I lay my head back against the wall and close my eyes. At first, there's nothing but darkness that I see, but then, out of nowhere, the girl from the gym pops into my mind. All I can think about is her body, how it felt against my palms. She's tall and thin with slight curves in all the right places. Her lips are full and pouty, her eyes a brilliant blue, and her hair is so dark brown, it's almost black. She's different than the girls I usually go after. She isn't sexy in an overt, obvious way and she hasn't tanned her skin to the point of it looking and feeling like leather. She's pale and soft. I bet she used to be goth in her younger years. I've never met a girl with skin that fair and hair that dark that didn't go through a goth phase in her youth.

My lips curl up at the corners while thinking about her accepting my invitation for a private lesson. I want my hands back on that body of hers. I want to be able to taste the sweat that drips onto those plump lips from working her so hard. My ears fill with the sounds of her grunts and whimpers that she let out as she punched the bag. My dick twitches when I think about being the one that makes her make those sounds.

I wish I would've caught her name. Or asked her out for a drink. But, like I said before, she's probably too shy to let loose with me. Then again, I like the chase, the waiting…the anticipation.

I'm sure she's the relationship type. She's gorgeous, but she's not easy. Usually, it's only the easy girls that take me up on my offer the first time it's given. I know one thing for sure: I'll be back at the gym every night until she shows up again.

———

I WAKE in the morning and dress for work. I step back and look myself over in the mirror. My new haircut with this suit doesn't look right. Usually, I keep my hair a bit longer, so I can style it. It really pulls the power suit thing together. But every year, around the time that I start training for the championship, I shave it off.

My work persona is a totally different me; it's the fake bullshit I put on to please my family. I'm not just some rich prick that sits in an office all day. I'm driven by danger and adrenaline. I need my heart pumping at full power to feel alive. And sitting behind a desk doesn't do that for me. However, if I didn't keep this part of my life, I'm sure I'd be disowned by my father. To him, a real man doesn't run around fighting. A real man sits behind his desk and gives orders, making others do his dirty work while he sits back and collects his money. My father hasn't seen the real me since I agreed to take over this company a little over a year ago. He doesn't know that I still box. He doesn't know that I race, or skydive, or anything but work for that matter.

I adjust my black tie and grab my briefcase. Heading down the stairs, I bump into Quinn again. She has her uniform unbuttoned a little more today. Maybe she picked up on my inner turmoil from last night regarding her. Either way, I'm a different me today. When I put on this suit, I'm not the man who has testosterone pumping through his veins from a good fight. This suit means I'm respected and feared and won't be controlled by my dick. It also means I'm a fake asshole. I'm getting sick of this game of pretend.

"Good morning, Mr. Windsor. Breakfast is ready for you in the dining room." She reaches out and takes my briefcase like every other morning.

I skip the pleasantries, offering only a small smile, and turn down the hall. Walking into the dining room and taking a seat at the table. I pick up my paper and read over it while she gets to work on pouring my coffee and making my plate.

"Is there anything else I can get for you?" she asks sweetly.

"No. Thank you," I clip out, picking up my coffee and taking a sip. The sweet mixture helps to ease the stress away—the stress that I put on with this suit.

She bows her head before leaving the room, leaving me in peace, just as I like it. I can't help but feel like I'm not the only one faking it. Quinn's sweetness seems a bit too much at times, like she's up to something.

As I read over the paper, I eat my eggs and bacon and drink my coffee. I glance at my watch to see that it's going on seven-thirty. I finish up and stand, heading for the door. She's already there waiting, holding my briefcase out for me to take. I've never asked her to pretend to be a fifties housewife and wait on me hand and foot. In fact, I've insisted she shouldn't, but it doesn't seem to get through to her.

"Thank you, Quinn." I take it from her, letting myself into the garage to get behind the wheel of my car.

When I get to the office, I take my private elevator directly to the top floor. I step off, and my secretary, Sarah, is already holding my door open with a cup of coffee in hand. "Good morning, sir."

I take the coffee and walk in with her following along behind me to read me my messages.

"Your sister called. She didn't say why she was calling but did request for you to call her back."

"Probably needs more money," I reply, shrugging out of my jacket and sitting down.

"Also, Callan called and said that he would be late for your golf game this morning. He had a late night and missed his flight home from Rio."

"Actually, can you call him back and cancel? I'm not in the mood to swing clubs today."

She nods. "Absolutely. Let me know if you need anything else."

"Sarah, I need last week's data reports."

"Of course." She walks out without another word.

Figuring I better call my sister back before she calls again, I pick up the phone.

"Hello?" she answers.

"Well, you're up early for an art student," I joke.

"Shut up. I'm not a student anymore. I graduated, remember?"

I laugh. "Did you though? Graduating means you don't have to be broke anymore, and you start making money. Are you doing that?"

"I have no idea why you're the favorite. You're such a dick."

"Probably because I have a job and don't keep asking Mom and Dad for money."

"I have a job!" she argues.

"Okay, what is it that you need?" I ask, waiting for the answer I already know is coming.

She lets out a long breath. "You're not going to make me say it, are you?"

"No fun in letting you weasel out of it," I say, smile stretching across my face.

"I need money, Bennet. My rent is due, and I can't swing it this month."

"That's what I thought." I laugh, and that causes her to breathe heavy into the phone. "I'll have Sarah send it to you by this afternoon."

"Thank you," she whispers, and I can hear the way her heart is breaking from having to say those words yet again.

"There's nothing wrong with saving your passion for your hobby, Val. I'm doing it."

"I'm not a sell-out, Bennet." Without another word, she hangs up the phone.

Is that what I am? Does she think I'm a sell out because I accepted Dad's offer to run his company? I'm making more than enough money to survive, and I still box and race. I don't think too long on the topic because I don't want to accept the truth that I *am* a fucking sellout.

Sarah walks back into the room. "Sir, the data reports are not ready. Brian has been out with the flu."

I let out a sigh and rub my eyes. "In this whole building, there's no one else that can write up a report? Find someone!" I yell, getting aggravated.

She nods, her gray hair falling into her eyes. "Yes, sir."

She leaves the room as quickly as she appeared.

It's only after I've scared her off that I realize that I forgot to ask her to send my sister money. Instead of going out there or calling her back in here, I type out a quick private message and send it directly to her computer.

After everything is set up, I move on to my messages, calling people back, reading and replying to emails, and generally kissing ass. I go over my schedule for the day and prepare for meetings. When I look up at the time, I see it's almost noon, and I still haven't gotten those data reports. I let out a deep breath and push the button that calls Sarah into my office.

"Yes, sir?" she asks, walking in.

"Reports?" I ask, sounding bored and tired of asking for them.

She nods in a hurry. "Yes, we finally found someone. A girl that's been waiting for the position to open up. She's working on them now and will have them up soon. Why don't you go have an early lunch, and I'll send her in as soon as you're back."

I nod, not trying to take my anger out on her. I know it's not her fault. "Okay, that's what I'll do. I'll be back in an hour. I have to present them to the board, Sarah; this isn't just a friendly request."

She smiles, I'm sure in her head she's telling me to eat shit and die, but instead she responds cheerfully, "Message received, Mr. Windsor. I promise to get them to you before close of business."

I leave the office the same way I came in, then walk through the garage to my car. The cloudy day has now turned to one of rain, so I quickly put the top up before leaving. Pulling up to my favorite restaurant, I greet Paolo, the owner. I'm in here often enough I have my own table, always ready for me. One of the perks of being a rich prick I suppose. "Ahh, Mr. Windsor! Greg, please," he says toward the bartender snapping his fingers. It's hardly a minute before an old fashioned is set down in front of me.

I pick up the glass and cheers to the Paolo and Greg. I tip it back and let the cool liquid spill into my mouth. It doesn't take long before a salmon steak is placed in front of me with an undressed salad. I like to keep it clean and lean while I'm training…apart from my occasional cocktail. I eat alone while reading over work documents on my phone. I finish off my drink and drop two hundred bucks on the table. I didn't ask for the wealth I have, but if I'm going to be a sellout, I might as well share it. I give a nod the staff and make my way back to the office, praying those damn reports are finished.

Walking back past Sarah, she opens the door and steps inside.

"I will call in Madeline, sir."

"Thank you." I shrug out of my jacket and sit behind my desk. The moment I turn for my computer, the doors are opening.

I look up and find the girl from the gym walking toward me with a file in hand.

3

MADDIE

I'm in my hole, sorting mail, when my manager walks up to me. "Today's your lucky day, Maddie."

I laugh. "Oh yeah? Did I drop my winning lottery ticket in the hallway again?" I laugh.

"Mr. Windsor is requesting the final financial reports for last quarter, and Brian, the guy that usually does them, has been out with the flu."

My head pops up, and my eyes grow wide. "Seriously? He's asking for me?"

She nods. "Well, he's asking to find someone that is qualified to do them. You're next in line. Let's go. You do know how to use Insight Analytics, correct? I saw it on your resume, but you never know if people are proficient."

"Yes, I'm fully proficient. I even have an advanced certification in analytics and analytic programs. It was kind of a big hobby of mine in school." I smile, but she doesn't seem amused at all.

She leads me to the office I've never been lucky enough to set foot in until now. She steps aside. "Here you are." She hands me a piece of paper with sign-on credentials, along with the outlined details of what is needed on the reports.

I take it from her with shaking hands. "Thank you."

"This is a very time-sensitive request. When you finish, take these directly to Mr. Windsor's office. His admin, Sarah, will take care of you when you get up there."

I nod. "I completely understand." This is the job I originally applied for when I got out of college, but at the time, there wasn't a spot open. However, they did offer me a spot in the mailroom, and I figured something is better than nothing. I was happy to have my foot in the door.

She walks out of the office and closes the door behind her. I take a seat at the computer and turn it on. Excitement bubbles in my stomach. I can't wait to show the CEO of Windsor Wealth Management what I can do. And hopefully, I can use it to leverage my worth to land my dream job and get out of that mailroom.

I finish up with my work a lot quicker than I anticipated. So instead of wasting time, I do a little extra. I generate a chart that shows how much the company spent last week on marketing our app, and how much it brought in. The company's newest effort was an app that, for a small monthly membership fee, helps manage smaller investments. It's a great opportunity for individuals to get their feet wet in investing and still feel they have complete control over how much they're vesting and diversifying.

The phone on the desk rings and I'm unsure whether or not I should answer it, then figure, why not?

"Madeline Strickland, data analysis," I answer just for fun, expecting the call to be for the usual person that's here.

"Madeline, would you mind bringing up the data reports, please?"

I smile at getting my first request. "Absolutely." I hang up the phone and make the journey to the top floor. The whole way, my palms are sweating, and my heart is racing. I give myself a pep talk. "This is it, Maddie. This is when the big boss gets to see all your hard work. You can do this. Keep calm and be confident. I totally nailed this request and went above and beyond. I am a valuable asset to this firm, and they are lucky to have me!" I punch my fist up in the air just as the chime sounds signaling my arrival.

The doors open, and I step off the elevator. As I approach the desk, a gray-haired woman stands and comes around the desk to greet me.

"Maddie? I'm Sarah. I assume you have the reports?"

I give her hand a quick squeeze and she ushers me toward the large doors of the office. I quickly thank her as I step into the biggest, fanciest office I've ever seen. The floor is made of black stone, with a rug the size of my apartment in the center. There's a seating area with black leather couches and a glass-top table between them.

I'm completely distracted by my surroundings, the massive floor-to-ceiling windows that overlook Chicago, the perfectly designed wall art that screams money.

I think my mouth is hanging open when I hear a throat-clearing cough behind me. I spin around to face the desk. The man behind it smiles at me, and I freeze.

Oh my god! It's the hot guy from the gym!

If I thought my heart was pounding before, it's nothing like now. I feel like it's about to rip straight through my chest. His eyes narrow with confusion. Maybe he doesn't remember me from the gym and he's just confused because I'm not the person that normally brings these up. I mean, I do look quite different in work clothes. Last night, I was in nothing but leggings and a sports bra.

Oh my God. My boss has seen me in a sports bra! My face reddens as I push myself forward.

"Hello, Mr. Windsor. It's nice to meet you. I'm Madeline Strickland. I'm the person they pulled to get you your reports." I hold out my hand, trying to pretend like I don't recognize him, trying to be professional.

He offers a small smile and shakes my hand. "Nice to meet you, Madeline."

"Please, call me Maddie." I hand him the file. "I know you do this every week, but I added in a few things that I thought might be helpful. I can explain them if you need."

"Okay, please do." He takes his seat and places the file on the desk.

I lean over and open it. "These top pages are what you receive every quarter, so I don't need to explain those. But I had some extra time and thought this could come in handy. This first page is what the company paid out last week with the new advertising campaign for the paid subscription app. This is what the company brought in with sales on the app."

He quirks an eyebrow, seemingly surprised by the numbers.

I flip to the next page. "This is how well your ads are doing. It seems to me that you are paying out a lot of money for this one and it's not bringing in half of what you spend." I point at a certain ad. "But this one, it seems to bring in steady income, and I think if you take the money from the first one and put it to the second, you'd more than double the income."

His lips part as he looks over the page.

"Finally," I flip to the last page. "This is a total count of how many hits your website got last week, and this is the final tally of how many of those hits turned into customers. I think with a new website design, you could put the information most people seem to be looking for regarding the app upfront, and you'd bring in more clients as well as app subscriptions."

"This is rather unusual, but also very interesting," he says, looking up at me.

I nod. "It is. I can't tell you how many times I've gotten on a website looking for something specific, got distracted by something else, and left the site without making a purchase. Most people seem to be more interested in info regarding turnout and profit rather than how the company was founded."

"This is amazing work, Maddie. Where is your normal department?" he asks, standing and towering over me.

I look up. "Ugh, I'm usually in the mailroom. I'm on hold for this position... for a year now, actually."

"We can't allow such talents to be wasted sorting mail. Let me contact your supervisor and see what I can do."

"Really? Well, what about the guy that's normally here?" I ask, pointing to the floor where I'm standing.

"He's not fired, if that's what you're thinking. Surely there's enough room in that office for two." His eyes stare at my feet and work their way up my body, just like last night.

Watching him look me up and down makes every muscle tighten. "Thank you, Mr. Windsor."

He smiles and holds out his hand. "Call me Bennet."

I nod and shake his hand. "Okay, Bennet. I better get back to work," I say, maintaining eye contact. I start walking backward and end up bumping my ass into the corner of a large chair. I let out a squeal and jump. "I'm sorry," I mutter, spinning around to watch where I'm going.

I open the door, and he stops me. "Oh, Madeline?"

"Yes?" I breathe out, too embarrassed to look him in the eye.

"I'll see you at the gym tonight."

With his words, my eyes jump up to his, and my mouth drops open. "I... I," I try again. Finally, I just shut my mouth, nod, and walk out.

Closing the door behind me, I stop and take a deep breath. It takes me several long seconds to calm down and notice his secretary is looking at me. I straighten up. "He's quite intimidating, isn't he?"

She offers a small smile and a nod.

I nod back then push forward, rushing to the elevator as quickly as I can.

———

I RUSH down to Jazz's office. I don't even knock. I just barge in, causing her to jump from her seat.

"Jeez, Maddie. You scared me to death!"

"I'm sorry. I just, I just left Mr. Windsor's office. You know him?"

She shakes her head. "I haven't had the pleasure of meeting him yet."

My eyes double in size. "He's the hot boxer from last night!"

Her brows skyrocket. "What?"

I nod as I fall into the empty seat across from her.

"Are you sure?" she asks, not knowing if she should take me seriously or not.

"Oh, I'm sure. I was trying to pretend like I didn't recognize him, but as I was walking out, he said, *see you at the gym tonight*," I say in a deeper voice.

She laughs. "He did not!"

"He did!" We both start laughing.

"It doesn't sound like much work is getting done in here," Damon says, walking in.

Jazz stands from her seat. "Maddie here was just telling me about the boxer from last night..." she glances at me, and I shake my head no.

"What about him?" Damon asks.

"Oh, I was just talking about going back tonight and taking him up on his offer of a private lesson." I grin as I stand up to leave.

"Gross, Maddie. I don't want to hear about your hook-ups." He turns his attention back to Jazz.

"Hey, one of your random hook-ups is now marrying you. And private boxing lesson isn't code for anything, Damon. So I don't want to hear it." I pull her door open and leave them behind me.

––––––––

WALKING BACK INTO THE GYM, I feel self-conscious. I go into the locker room and lock up my bag and jacket. I look myself over in the mirror and suddenly worry that my gray leggings were a mistake, I'm going to sweat right through them and look like I peed myself. But there's nothing I can do about it now. I shake my insecurities from my head and push open the door, walking out into the main gym.

I jump on the treadmill and run a mile, needing a warm-up. Finally, I open the door to where the ring is. It squeaks and all four men to look up at me from what they were doing. I almost want to stop and turn around right then, but I tell myself to keep going.

I walk across the floor, pulling my gloves on as I pick my bag for the evening. I tune everyone out and focus on the tips Bennet gave me last night about keeping my wrist straight and putting all my body weight into my punches. I hit the bag over and over, and just when I'm wrapping up, I spin around to find Bennet standing off to the side, watching me.

He has his arms crossed over his chest, his green eyes locked on me. His lips are turned up into a small smile. "Very good, Madeline," he says, walking over.

The room we're in is an add-on to the regular gym. It's just bare wood framing with sheet metal keeping the room enclosed. Fluorescent lights are secured to each rafter, meaning it's not completely lit up. There's a spot of light, a gap of darkness, and then another spot of light. As he walks closer to me, he moves in and out of the light. When he steps into the darker areas, he appears dangerous yet sexy. His muscles are rippling, and his jaw is tensed. His eyes darken as he walks closer and takes me in.

"Thank you, Mr. Windsor, and it's Maddie. You can call me Maddie," I nearly spit out, a little annoyed that this hot guy I've been fantasizing about having a fling with is now my boss.

He shakes his head. "I'm not the guy you saw in the office when I'm here. When I'm here, I'm just Bennet. I'm not your boss."

I nod once, looking at my feet. "You are my boss, though."

"Are you the same person out of work that you are at work?" he asks, finally coming to a stop a foot away from me.

I nod. "Pretty much. What you see is what you get."

He chuckles under his breath. "I know that isn't true. If I'd just run into you at the office, I never would've guessed that you'd be into boxing. And I'm sure you have a few more passions hidden away." His voice is deep and raspy. Just listening to him talk turns me on. A light sweat prickles my skin, and I find myself reaching for something to say. Right now, all I want to do is agree with everything he's saying and hope he takes me into the ring where we can claim it as our own.

I force a smile. "I guess you'll never know." I start removing my gloves.

"You showed up tonight for your private lesson. That has to mean something."

I nod. "I have to admit, I was hoping there was a bit of an innuendo with your offer, but then I found out that you're my boss. That no longer seems like a good idea."

"I told you, I'm not your boss here."

I bite my lower lip. "So, what? At night you're going to be Bennet, the boxer that trains me and gives me "private lessons," and during the day, you're going to be Mr. Windsor, the guy that assigns me jobs and writes me up when I can't meet those impossibly high standards? Sounds like a trashy made-for-tv movie."

He turns his head to the side and lets out a deep laugh.

I laugh. "I didn't mean to say that out loud." I feel my face heat up and know that it's bright red.

"Let's just take it one day at a time. See where it goes, huh?" He's wearing his panty-dropping smile, and his green eyes are lit up from laughing. As much as I want to say no, we can't do this, I can't deny my desires.

I smile and nod. "Alright, Bennet. Train me."

His eyes flash to the ring. "Get those gloves back on and let's go." He starts toward the ring.

I walk over, pulling my gloves on. He hops up into the ring and pulls apart the ropes, allowing me to slide in. He picks up some padded gloves and puts them on.

"I know you can hit a bag that stays still; let's see how you do with something that moves." He stands, bouncing up and down on his toes, moving his hands for me to punch. I crack my neck and put up my fists.

"Come on, Maddie. Let's see what you can do."

4

BENNET

I have to admit, the harder I work her, the more she gets under my skin. She's toned and tough, and she doesn't quit easily. I've watched her since she walked in. She's been working for two hours now and shows no signs of quitting. She doesn't stop to catch her breath; she doesn't complain that she's too hot or tired. She just keeps pushing, and that, to me, is a total turn-on.

Finally, I call it quits, and she collapses on the ring floor. I stand back, watching as the sweat beads up on her skin. Her chest is rising and falling quickly, and her toned stomach teases me with every breath.

"Tired?" I ask, holding out my hand.

She takes it, and I pull her up. She stumbles, falling against my chest. I look down, and she looks up. Our eyes lock as her lips part. There's a pull between us, something that is begging me to lean in and feel her lips with mine. My tongue comes out and wets my lips, preparing for the kiss.

She blinks, and the moment is gone. Her hands squeeze my biceps as she steadies herself. "I'm sorry. I just got a little light-headed," she says as she pulls away.

I release her and step back, needing to put some distance between us since she doesn't seem ready to step forward with me. "You need to get something to eat and rest. You took a lot out of your body today. I'd suggest an Epsom salt bath, add ice if you can stand it."

She nods and wipes the sweat from her brow. "Thanks for the private lesson, Bennet." She starts ripping off her gloves.

"No problem," I reply, walking to the side of the ring and pulling open the ropes for her.

"Same time tomorrow?" she asks.

I nod, locking my eyes with hers.

She offers up a grin, steps out of the ring, and walks away without another word. I can't do anything but stand there and watch her go. There's something about her that I can't shake. She's gorgeous; there's no denying that. Maybe it's the fact that I can't just reach out and take her like I can with almost any other woman. Most women that I sleep with only have one thing on their mind: a wedding ring. They don't care if we have a connection. They just want a chance at living out the rest of their lives in ease—something money like mine provides. But Maddie, she's different. She doesn't look at me and see dollar signs; at least, I don't think she does. The first night, she looked at me with pure, unadulterated lust. A stranger she wanted that could give her body pleasure without apology. But now, she looks at me and sees him, the guy I am during the day. And I hate that. I have to get her to see there's more to me than a suit and a big office. I have to get her to let her guard down to see me the way she saw me last night.

I let out a deep breath and shake my head as I step out of the ring. Heading back to the locker room, I bump into Phillip.

"She came back for that private lesson, huh?"

I laugh. "Yeah, but I ran into her today… at work."

"Oh, fuck. That complicates things."

I nod. "Yup."

"So, what's the next step?"

"The next step?" I ask him, turning to see him sit down on the bench.

"Well, there's a next step, isn't there. A way to get her to forget that you're her boss? A way to get her to cut loose and have fun and enjoy being your plaything?" He smirks.

I roll my eyes and shake my head. "She's not just my plaything. I mean, yeah, I want to start something up with this woman, but…" My sentence drops off.

"But nothing. All you want to do is have a fling with her for a couple months and move on to the next one. Same thing you always do, bro."

"No, that's not it at all. It can last more than a few months. I don't want as many women as I can get. Really, I just want one. One woman that is okay with having two separate lives. She lives her way, I live mine, and then we meet in the middle. I don't want marriage and kids and happily ever after. I just want to enjoy my life and have fun. Why's that so hard? Why do women have to complicate that?"

He shrugs as he picks up his wedding band and slides it into place. "Marriage isn't that bad. It's kind of nice. It's like having your best friend with you at all times, someone that is always on your side and has your back. Oh, and sex whenever I want it." He sticks his tongue out as he flips me off.

I scoff. "I have my own back. And don't act like for one second you demand sex and get it. We both know you don't wear the pants in your marriage," I tell him, closing my locker and walking out.

———

BY THE TIME I get to leave the office on Tuesday, I'm amped up for the gym. I can't wait to get her alone. I can't wait to have an excuse to put my hands on her body. And I can't wait to see if tonight will be the night I get her to let her guard down.

I walk into the gym and find her jabbing away at the punching bag. Tonight, she's wearing a pair of shorts. They're black and So. God. Damn. Short. They fit tightly and end just under her ass. If I hadn't seen these shorts around the gym before, I'd say they were underwear. Just looking at her tight ass in those shorts makes my mouth water.

"Ready?" I ask, stepping up behind the bag.

She nods. "Let's do it."

I smirk and send her a wink. "Let's do it."

She laughs and shakes her head. "You know, you don't have to do that—the whole double-meaning thing. If you have something on your mind, say it."

"Okay," I say, stepping into the ring and pulling open the ropes. "Why don't you let me take you back to my place where I can spend the rest of the night between those legs, worshiping your body?"

She smiles, trying to cover the slight bit of shock registering across her face. "I would, but I wouldn't know who'd I'd be sleeping with. Would it be Bennet or Mr. Windsor?" Her brows arch high, and her smile turns into a full-on grin.

I shake my head. "Whichever you prefer, Maddie."

She laughs and puts her fists in the air. "It's not going to happen, Bennet."

I hold up my hand, and she takes the hit. "You like the chase, don't you? You could give in, and you know you'd enjoy it, but holding out, punishing the both of us, it's more fun for you."

She shrugs one shoulder and hits the pad again. "I can't deny that I like watching you beg."

I laugh. "Who's begging? You wanted honesty, and I gave it to you."

She takes a step toward me and hits again. "You want honesty?" This time, she does a quick combo, hitting with both fits. "I'd love for you to take me back to your place. I want to see you moving above me, feel you inside me, but then, it'd end, and we'd go back to work where I'm treated cold and like any other employee. I like Bennet. Mr. Windsor, I'm not too fond of." She swings to punch again, but this time, I dodge her hit and grab her around her waist, pulling her against me. My mouth lands on hers, and instead of pushing me away, she wraps her legs around my hips and her arms around my neck, accepting the kiss. As her tongue twists with mine I completely forget that we're in public.

Her lips are softer than I ever could've imagined. Her tongue tastes of a sweetness I can't place, maybe a flavor that's all her own.

And the way her body fits perfectly against mine, it causes me to lose my head completely. I was just wanting to kiss her, a little taste to see what she's missing, but her reaction made me get lost. I'm wrapped in her completely, and there's no way I can stop myself. If she lets me, I'll fuck her right here, right now. There's no going back.

I grind my hips against her core, and she lets out a whimper, a soft sound that cuts right through me. When my lips leave hers to travel down her neck, she lets her head roll back and lets out a long breath.

"Bennet, we have to stop," she says, pushing against my shoulders.

Somehow, I pull away, studying her face.

"This wasn't supposed to happen. We're not Bennet and Maddie. We're Mr. Windsor and Madeline." She scoots away from under me and leaves the ring. I fall back onto my ass and watch as she exits the boxing area completely. She never looks back. The sound of the big metal door slamming is like a slap in the face, like I've been doused in cold water.

I let myself fall back, only seeing the lights hanging on the ceiling.

"She walked out on you?"

I lift my head to see Phillip leaning against the ring. My head falls back. "She's going to fucking kill me."

He laughs. "Mark my words, she's going to be the one you end up with."

"What?" I ask as he turns to leave.

He doesn't answer me. He just keeps walking.

"Hey! What did you say?" I ask again.

But again, nothing. He opens the door to the locker room and slides inside, leaving me alone.

"Fuck," I whisper, letting my head fall back against the floor.

———

"Sarah, please call Madeline to my office," I say, releasing the intercom button.

"Will do, sir," she replies.

It's only a second later when she comes back on the line. "Ms. Strickland is out sick today, sir."

Out sick, huh? I highly fucking doubt it. No doubt, I scared her off. She's probably pissed at me. Not for kissing her, but for making her realize how badly she wants me. It's easy to avoid something when you don't allow it to come close enough. But the closer you get, the harder it is to resist. Last night, I got too close. Too close to deny, anyway.

I open the company directory and find her number. For the first time, it dawns on me. Her name is Madeline Strickland. Fuck, same last name as Damon. Damon, a friend I've had for many years now. A friend that's helped me out of many jams. A guy that I call anytime I need something. Fuck, this just got a lot more difficult. Are they related? I know he'd briefly mentioned having a sister, but I never heard him say her name. Should I talk to him about seeing her? I mean, that would be the respectful thing to do, wouldn't it? But right now, she doesn't want to see me. She's avoiding me. Maybe I shouldn't count my chickens before they hatch. I mean, if I smooth things over and we start to move forward, that's when I need to talk to Damon.

Quickly, I pick up the phone and call her.

"Hello?" she answers, using a fake sick voice.

"Why aren't you at work?" I ask.

I hear her let out a long breath. "I just needed time."

"Time to what?" I demand.

"Time to work through what happened between us. Time to sort through it all. I don't want to be sleeping with my boss, Bennet."

"Then don't sleep with your boss. Sleep with your boxing coach." I smirk, forgetting that she can't see me.

"I'll be back in the office tomorrow. See you then."

"Wait, you're skipping the gym tonight?"

"I think it's for the best; don't you?"

"No! No, I don't think it's for the best. I think you need to stop hiding. It's obvious that I'm feeling something for you, and you haven't tried very hard to hide what you're feeling for me. Why are you making this so complicated?"

"Goodbye, Mr. Windsor." Without another word, she hangs up, and that pisses me off.

I hang up the phone, copy down her address, and stand from my desk. As I'm walking out, I say, "Sarah, cancel the rest of my meetings for the day. I'm leaving the office."

I drive over to her apartment and wait outside until someone walks out. I catch the door and slip my way inside. I find her apartment and knock on the door.

"Mrs. Windle, I already told you I don't have any sugar," she says from the inside.

I knock again.

"I don't have any milk, bread, or honey either. I don't shop. I just live here."

I want to laugh, but I knock again.

This time, she opens it. Annoyance is clearly written on her face but seeing me makes her freeze. "Wh—what are you doing here?" Her brows pull together as her eyes narrow at me.

"I have something to show you. Can I come inside?"

She lets out a deep breath but steps to the side and opens the door wider.

I take a few steps inside and turn to face her. "It doesn't matter what's going on with me; don't skip work because of it. I don't want you feeling out of place at your job."

She crosses her arms over her chest. "It's good to see you again, Mr. Windsor. How's Bennet doing?" She walks past me into the living room.

I follow after her. "This isn't a boss or coach thing. It's just how it is. If we're going to be two separate people, you can't let Bennet from last night affect your work with Mr. Windsor today, and vice versa. Got it?"

She shakes her head. "I'm not doing anything with either of you. God, do you know how crazy this sounds? I feel like I have to have a split personality just to keep up with you."

I nod once. "I do. I've had some fucked-up stuff in life, and this is the only way I've found I can manage to live."

"Why? Please, explain this to me so that maybe I can understand."

I'm not exactly the type to spill my guts to someone I barely know but fuck it...there's something about Maddie that compels me to be open and honest with her.

I sit on the coffee table in front of her. "I was raised...privileged. In my teenage years, I did whatever I wanted, and when I got into trouble, my dad paid my way out of it. That didn't stop when I got into college. By then, I wasn't a very good guy. I bought expensive sports cars and raced them. I took up boxing and started competing. I found the only way I can feel alive, to feel like this life actually means something, is to get an adrenaline rush. Live dangerously. So, the last race I was in, the guy I was racing wrecked his car and died. It wasn't my fault. I didn't do anything to cause him to wreck, but he did. And his family found out I was involved. They saw dollar signs. They sued, and my dad, doing what he always did, paid them off. He then told me that if I wanted to continue to live like that, I would be cut off. I could do whatever I wanted, but the next time I got into trouble or needed help of any kind, I'd be on my own. Or, he said I could straighten up and take his place at the company. I thought about it and decided to choose the latter.

"I took his place at the company and turned my whole life around. But after a few months, I felt like I was dying. I felt tied down, like I was suffocating. I knew I had to do something. Working at the company, it wasn't living. So, I decided to be Mr. Windsor at work, the son my father wants, and I would go back to being Bennet on my time off. It was the only way I could do what needed to be done and still feel alive."

She nods her head, understanding. "I get it, Bennet. I do. But I can't do that. I can't be one person here and another person there."

"I'm not asking you to. I'm asking that when you see me at work, to see me, not the guy in a suit that has no sense of purpose. See me, Maddie. The guy that's standing in front of you right now. Do I need to lose the suit for you to see him?" I stand and rip off my jacket. Next comes the tie and the shirt. I toss it all into the floor and hold my hands out at my sides. "Is this better? If you want to get to know me first, that's fine. But this is the me you need to know. Not him." I point at the dress clothes on the floor.

"I'm crazy and passionate. I have fun. I live life to the fullest, and all I'm asking is for a little bit of your time. Just get to know me and forget all about that dick at the office," I plead.

5

MADDIE

I can't deny that I find him attractive. Okay, more like drop-dead sexy to the point that I can't close my eyes without seeing him. And if I'm honest with myself, I do want to get to know him. I guess if we started hanging out, it would be casual, and I wouldn't want anyone from work knowing about it anyway, so it would be on the down-low. We'd have to keep up appearances. So, would taking this step forward with him be that big of a deal?

"What is it that you want from me, Bennet? I'm not a relationship girl."

"That's fine with me. I'm not the type of man you marry anyway," he jokes, sitting back on the table in front of me. "I just want to take you out, get to know you, have fun, and have someone to enjoy things with."

I bite my lower lip and nod. "Okay. We'll be friends outside of work, but this is just between us. I don't want anyone thinking that I'm sleeping my way to the top or something. At work, it's Madeline and Mr. Windsor only," I say emphatically. I don't want him blurring the lines.

"Deal," he agrees with a smile.

It's contagious, and I smile back.

"I guess I can put my clothes back on now," he laughs, standing up and retrieving his clothes.

"What was it that you wanted to show me?" I ask, walking him back to the door. "Surely it wasn't your chest."

He laughs and shakes his head. "I'll show you tomorrow at the office. It can wait."

I nod. "Okay." I open the door, and he starts stepping out.

Suddenly, he turns back toward me. "Can I take you out to dinner tonight?"

"Before or after the gym?" I ask, leaning against the door frame with my arms crossed.

"You're going to the gym?"

I shrug and offer a half-smile. "Why not?"

"After," he answers, turning and leaving.

———

THE WORKOUT he puts me through is hot and tiring, but it ends quickly, and we each go to the locker rooms to shower and get ready for dinner. I wash up and dry off. Since I didn't bring my entire bathroom with me, I braid my hair and let it hang over my shoulder. Then I pull on a pair of yoga pants and a long-sleeve Henley shirt. I don't even bother trying to put on makeup. When I exit the locker room, Bennet is leaning against the counter, talking with another guy and waiting on me.

"Hey," I say, coming to a stop next to him.

"Hey." He stands upright. "Are you ready?"

I nod as I check him out. He's wearing a pair of fitted dark-wash jeans and a t-shirt that stretches over his muscled arms and chest. He looks downright mouthwatering, and here I am in yoga pants and a crappy shirt.

God, I hope we're not going someplace nice.

"This way," he says, placing his hand on my lower back as he leads me out of the gym and into the parking lot.

He opens the passenger side door on a black convertible Mercedes

AMG and motions for me to climb inside. I don't know much about cars, but I know enough to conclude that this car is not only expensive, but custom.

"So, this is your car, huh?" I ask, walking slowly around it.

He nods with a smile. "Yeah. What did you expect?"

I laugh and shrug. "I don't know. I guess I never pictured it, but it makes sense." I take my seat, and he closes the door. He climbs behind the wheel and starts the car; the engine roars to life and settles into a purr. He shifts into gear and hits the gas.

As we drive through the city, I look around: at him, at the car, just mesmerized by it all.

"Why are you staring?" he asks with a grin.

I laugh and shrug. "I don't know. I was just thinking that this car is more Mr. Windsor than Bennet."

"Oh yeah? What do you think Bennet should drive?"

Again, I shrug. "I don't know. Something big. A guy in a suit fits in this car. A bad-ass boxer, he needs a Hummer or something big and awesome but still expensive and fancy."

He laughs. "Okay, tomorrow, I'll go buy a Hummer."

I smack his arm. "No, I was just being stupid and talking. Don't go buy an expensive vehicle on my behalf." I look around and see that we're leaving the city. "Where are we going?"

"My place," he says with a smile, wagging his brows.

"Bennet, seriously, I'm not sleeping with you. We're friends. That's it."

He laughs. "I'm not bringing you here to take advantage of you. I'm bringing you here for the dinner my staff has already prepared. It's not like either of us are dressed for someplace fancy, and we both just kicked our own asses at the gym."

I turn my head and look at the massive houses we're driving past, feeling a little guilty for jumping to conclusions.

When he pulls into a driveway with brick walls and an iron gate, I look forward, hoping to catch a peek of the house. He puts in a code, and the gates open. The driveway is long and winding, with big trees and bushes and flowers covering the grounds. Finally, a big, three-story mansion comes into view. It has everything, from the circle drive down to the fountain in the center.

I laugh. "God, do all you rich people pick your houses out of a magazine, or what?"

He grins. "I know, it does look very—"

"Ridiculous?" I finish for him.

He shrugs. "I admit, it is a tad wasteful."

"A tad?" I ask.

"Okay, so I don't get any bonus points for the house. I got it." He opens my door, and I step out.

"I don't give bonus points for material things, Bennet."

He closes my door and takes my arm, leading me toward the front door. "Noted." Even though he doesn't sound happy, he still smiles and winks.

When he walks me into the foyer, my mouth nearly drops open, and my eyes feel like they bug out of my skull.

"You're not impressed; don't make that face, Maddie," he tells me, dropping his bag on the floor by the door.

I laugh. "I'm amazed, but not impressed."

"Let me guess, you don't get impressed by material things either," he teases.

I don't answer because he pulls me across the room and down a hallway to the dining room. The table is already set, two glasses of wine poured. He pulls out my chair, and I sit down. He joins me and holds up his glass of wine. We cheers, and I take a sip, wrinkling my nose.

"What's wrong?"

I place the glass back on the table. "I'm more of a beer girl."

He holds up his finger as he stands and leaves the room. A second later, he's coming back with two beers in his hand. "Better?" he asks, handing one over.

I smile and take it. "Much." I twist off the top and take a long drink.

He shakes his head. "You're much different than I thought you'd be."

"How so?"

He takes a drink and sets it on the table, giving me his full attention. "Well, most women, even if they don't know this side of things, they still try to act like they do. They complement things like the vase in the hallway, something that looks expensive, but still, something they know nothing about it. You," he points at me. "You haven't done any of that."

I take another drink and lock my eyes on his. "Well, first, I don't agree with the most women comment; perhaps it's the women you're choosing. As for pretending, what's the point? Things and money don't do it for me, Bennet. Being a good person, treating others with kindness, helping when someone needs help—those are things that impress me. Anyone can have money and act like a rich asshole. It's those that choose to be a good person that I like. You could be dirt poor, but as long as I enjoy your company, I'd like you just the same."

He smiles. "I've never met a woman like you."

"There's a first time for everything." I hold up my bottle, and he clinks his against it.

As we eat, I can see him loosening up. For the first time since I met him, he lets everything fall away. He doesn't bring up work or money or boxing or his family. We just talk about music, movies, books, and things we like to do. I learn that he likes to do anything dangerous: rock climbing, skydiving, racing his car at the speed of light. And I tell him that I would love to do all of those things. Well, except the racing part, but I'd love to watch. He asks about where and how I grew up and shows interest in how I got into the field I did. By the time we're done with dinner and dessert, I feel like I know him on a whole different level, like he's a friend.

"What do you say to watching a movie and having a few more drinks?" he asks, picking up my hand that's on the table and holding it.

I look at his hand on mine. "I don't know. It's getting pretty dark, and I don't want to make you drive me home super late."

"It wouldn't be an imposition at all," he insists. "Or you can just stay the night." His smile grows bigger.

I shake my head. "Really, I should be going." I place my cloth napkin onto the table and stand.

"If you insist, but I was planning on watching *Death Becomes Her.*" He grins, knowing that's my all-time favorite movie because we had just talked about it.

I laugh. "Fine, one movie."

He holds up his hands, palms facing me.

He shows me to the living room and excuses himself to get the movie and a few more beers. When he comes walking back in a few moments later, he has a small cooler that's filled with ice and beer.

"You really go all out, don't ya?" I ask, grabbing a beer and opening it.

He shrugs as he bends down and puts in the movie. "I hate getting up when I'm watching a movie."

"Me too," I agree, happy that he's not the type that wants to stop the movie every fifteen minutes to use the bathroom, get drinks or snacks.

He comes back to the couch and sits down next to me. Suddenly, we feel very close, which is weird because we've been closer before. But this is different. This is intimate and relaxing. I've already had two beers with dinner, and now I'm on my third. Everything is starting to sound like a good idea, even though, in the back of my head, I know it's not.

His scent makes its way to my nose and causes me to sink into the couch in relaxation. I can feel his heat radiating off of him. It soaks into me and makes me feel comfortable yet amped and ready to go at the same time. When his hand bumps mine, it feels like it's been burned, but it's a burn I love. A burn I'm suddenly wanting to feel more of. But I tell myself it's just the alcohol, and to focus on the movie.

Turns out, what I focus on is the beer, because before the movie is even halfway over, I've had two more. My vision is starting to blur around the edges, and everything is funny. When his hand bumps against mine again, I turn and look at him. He's engrossed in the movie, so for a split second, I get to see him. Just him. No walls up, no expectations to meet, nobody to impress. It's just him, carefree and laid back. I don't think I've ever seen him this relaxed.

"What?" he asks, noticing that I'm staring at him.

I smile and shake my head. "I've never seen you so laid back. For once, it looks like you're not carrying the weight of the world on your shoulders."

He looks at me with heavy eyes. "It's because I'm with you. For the first time, I don't have to worry about meeting expectations, or being a certain version of myself. I can just be me: the me I hide from everyone else."

Something about his honesty calls to me. Maybe being with him wouldn't be such a bad idea. I mean, we both know we're not looking to settle down. We're just looking for someone special to share things with, be with.

Without saying a word, I crawl into his lap. He watches me with unsure eyes, but he doesn't say anything. Slowly, I lean forward and press my lips to his. He kisses me back, soft and slow. Then pulls away and looks into my eyes.

"Do you do this with all your friends?" He tries to keep a straight face but fails.

"Nope. Guess you're special," I whisper, moving back in for a kiss.

This time, he's much more prepared, and he kisses me back, hard and fast. His hand squeezes my hips and slowly moves up and down my back. I reach down in between us, grabbing his shirt and pulling it upward. Our kiss breaks for only a second until he's free of his shirt, and then our lips are back, moving along with each other.

With his shirt now gone, he lays me back on the couch, covering my body with his. His lips start moving down my jaw and then to my neck. His hands on my hips start moving upward, pushing my shirt up my body as he goes. Every muscle tightens when his hands find my flesh. They're warm and strong, not too smooth but not too rough. You can tell he likes working with his hands.

I'm completely lost in the way his body feels against mine, so when he pulls away, I'm shocked. He sits up and shakes his head, rubbing his eyes.

I sit up. "What's wrong?" I ask, breathless, my heart still reeling.

"You didn't want this earlier."

"I know."

"Why now?" He looks at me, and his green eyes are practically glowing.

I shrug. "I don't know. It just felt right. I've gotten to know you better, learned why you are the way you are. And you've shown me that there's more to you than just work and boxing. I got to see you let your guard down. I just feel closer to you."

He nods, and the seriousness on his face eases away. "It has nothing to do with how much we've had to drink tonight? Because I want you, Maddie. I do, but not this way."

I lick my lips. "If I said the alcohol had nothing to do with it, I'd be lying. But I wouldn't blame it on being drunk either. Yes, it's loosened me up some. It helped me to let go of everything that was holding me back earlier."

"As much as I want this, I think we should get you home. I like getting what I want, but I don't want to cheat to do it." He stands and adjusts himself before holding out his hand to me.

I place mine in his, and he pulls me up. "It isn't cheating, Bennet. But I respect your decision."

He places his hands on either side of my face and pulls me against him. I think he's going to kiss me, but he just locks his eyes on mine. "I want you, but I want you to want me back when you're sober. I don't want you to need a few drinks in to loosen you up. I want you to want me every moment of every day. And I'll wait as long as I need to until that happens."

I smile at his words. "Okay," I agree.

He closes the small gap between us and gives me a soft, slow kiss.

"Come on. I'll have my driver take you home."

He releases me, all but one hand, and he leads me through the house and into the garage where we climb into the back of a blacked-out town car.

As we wait for the driver, he takes my hand in his and holds it between us. "There is a function that I have to go to for work. It's a formal event, and I need a date. Would you like to go with me?"

"I thought we said this was just an outside-of-work thing? I don't want it get—"

"Nobody from work will be there. Nobody who knows you anyway," he interrupts. "As CEO of the company, I have to make an appearance for a charity event. It will be a bunch of old board members and stuffy rich people." He smiles.

I look over at him in the darkness. "Would I be going with you or with Mr. Windsor?"

He moves his head from side to side. "I guess a little of both. I can be carefree when it's just you and me, but out there, I have a reputation to uphold."

I nod and offer up a small smile. It's too bad that he thinks he can't be himself around anyone else. It must get tiring to constantly pretend to be something you're not.

"I'd love to go with the both of you," I joke.

6

BENNET

My driver pulls up to the curb at her apartment building, and as she prepares to leave the car, I pull her in for one last kiss. I hate myself for stopping us earlier. There's nothing I want more than to slide deep inside her. But I want her to want it as badly as I do. I want her to need it. And I'm more than willing to wait. Something about her calls to me in a way no other woman has. I've never had to work for women before, and the fact that she's making me work for it is a turn-on in itself. I want her. But I want to deserve her. And I know that I don't yet.

Her lips move softly against mine, and her tongue teases my senses. I have the urge to pull her on top of me and take what I wouldn't earlier, but I force myself to let her go.

"Goodnight, Madeline," I whisper against her lips.

She smiles. "Goodnight, Bennet." She climbs out, and I watch her until she gets into the building.

———

I WAKE in the morning and get to the office quickly. I respond to emails and phone messages for the first hour, then decide to look for

Maddie. I walk out of my office, and Sarah looks up at me from her desk.

"Sarah, could you please tell me where I can find Madeline Strickland?"

She nods. "Of course, sir." She sits down and starts tapping around on her computer. "Third floor, room three-seventeen."

"Thank you," I say, pushing forward.

I get in the public elevator and push the button for the third floor. It stops on the fifth floor, and someone else gets on. At first, he pays me no mind, but then it dawns on him, and he gives me a double-take.

"Excuse me," he says.

I look up and meet his eyes. "Yes?"

"You're Mr. Windsor, right?"

I nod. "I am."

"It's nice to meet you, sir. I'm Kevin. I've worked here for about four years now."

I shake his hand. "It's nice to meet you, Kevin. What is it that you do here?"

"I work in HR," he tells me just as the elevator doors open on the third floor.

I point out of the elevator. "This is my floor. It was nice to meet you, and thank you for all your hard work."

"Thank you, sir," he says excitedly as he steps back for me to get off.

As I leave the elevator, I think back on that conversation, and for the life of me, I can't remember ever having a conversation like that before. I've never met the majority of my employees. Hell, I use a private elevator to avoid them. Why do I do that? Why am I so insistent on following in my father's footsteps? Maybe spending all this time with Maddie is changing me. She said she likes good people. Maybe I'm changing for her. But I don't feel as if I'm forcing myself to do so.

I walk into room three-seventeen and find Maddie sitting at a computer. Across the room from her is another man, Brian, who usually provides me with my quarterly analytics.

"Ms. Strickland?" I ask, getting both of their attention.

Her head pops up, and her eyes lock on mine. "Mr. Windsor?" she asks with a smile playing on her lips.

I turn and look at Brian. "Would you excuse us for a moment?"

He nods. "Absolutely, Mr. Windsor." He stands and walks out of the room, closing the door behind him.

"How's your day?" I ask, walking across the room.

"Good. How's yours?" She stands up behind her desk.

"Much better now," I reply, leaning in for a kiss.

But instead of kissing me, she places one finger on my chest and pushes me back. "Why is Bennet here? Where's Mr. Windsor?" She quirks an eyebrow.

I laugh. "He left with Brian," I tell her, reaching for her, but she steps back.

"We can't do this here, Bennet."

"Why not? Nobody will know," I try.

"I bet they're all out there right now, talking about how Mr. Windsor gave me such a big promotion and now he's in here alone with me."

I wave my hand in the air. "Who cares what they think?"

"I do. I have to work with these people," she says, crossing her arms over her chest.

"Alright, I'm sorry. I didn't know you were so serious at work."

She smiles slightly. "At work, you're Mr. Windsor, and I'm Ms. Strickland. The end. Got it?"

I nod. "I got it."

"And if you need something from me, call me to your office. Don't come to mine," she insists.

"Okay," I agree, standing up straight. "I do have something to show you, though."

"Okay, I'll be up after lunch," she says, sliding back into her chair.

I'm left a little speechless. I'm used to getting whatever the hell I want, especially when it comes to women.

I nod as I walk out of the room, a little confused. Though I like that she's strong-willed and doesn't melt at my feet.

———

LUNCH ROLLS AROUND, and I want to ask Maddie to join me, but after the talk she gave me earlier, I'm a little afraid. Instead of asking her or going out alone, I have Sarah call me something in. I sit at my desk and eat my salmon salad while watching boxing matches on YouTube. It makes my muscles burn to get back to the gym. I feel like I haven't worked out in a week. Training Maddie is a lot less strenuous than my usual workout. I think tonight, I'll go early so I can get my workout in before she gets there.

At one o'clock on the dot, my doors open and in walks Maddie.

"Sorry to come in unannounced, but your secretary wasn't at her desk." She points toward the door behind her.

"She's still on lunch. She takes an extra twenty minutes. She needs it, putting up with me all this time."

She laughs. "That poor woman needs more than twenty minutes. She needs a paid week-long vacation!" Her eyes grow wide, and it makes me laugh.

"Yeah, yeah. Come here," I tell her, loading the screen on the computer. "This is our new company site."

"What? You did it?" she asks, excited that I listened to her advice. Her eyes are lit up, and her smile is wide.

"I did. Check it out." I stand and let her take my seat.

She sits down and scrolls through the page, clicking on certain things. She looks over her shoulder at me. "I can't wait to get back to my desk to compare the numbers. This is exciting!"

I laugh. "I think you're the easiest woman in the world to please."

Her smile is still in place as she nods her head up and down. "This is great. I'm going back to my desk." She stands. "Do you want me to send you the numbers when I'm done? They'll be super preliminary since this is a new change. I'd recommend at least thirty days of data to truly start measuring the metrics."

"Absolutely," I say, grabbing ahold of her wrist to stop her from walking away.

I pull her to my chest, and our eyes meet. "Nobody can see what we're doing now," I point out.

Her eyes fall from mine for a second before coming right back. "You're right." She leans forward and presses her mouth to mine. Finally, with her lips on mine for the first time today, I feel like I can breathe. Air rushes into my lungs as a tingle takes over my body. I live in this kiss, wanting it to last forever.

All too soon, she pulls away. "I'll see you at the gym tonight, Bennet."

I can't say anything. All I can do is watch her go while talking myself out of pulling her back.

7

MADDIE

Seeing his hard chest that has sweat dripping over every muscle is my kryptonite. It does me in, pushes me over the edge. Seals my fate. Whatever happens between us, it's going to stay in this moment. I'm no longer going to deny myself something I so desperately want.

When I'm down on my knees in front of him, I can't help but to open my eyes and look up his hard body. I see nothing but waves of muscles as he lets his head fall back against the wall, his jaw tensed and Adam's apple bobbing. When I push him far back in my throat, he lets out this moan that tells me I'm doing everything exactly right.

He places his hand on my jaw, gently urging me backward. I look up at him, and his green eyes burn. Without missing a beat, he picks me up against him and presses my back against the wall. Our mouths meet as he uses his hand to guide himself into me. The second he's inside, I suck in a deep breath. I feel whole having him there.

I've heard people talk about finding the one, and I always thought they were full of shit. I never felt like I was missing something. I've always felt whole on my own. But the minute he claims me, *whole* has a whole new meaning. Now, I'm whole, with him inside me.

He moans against my lips as he slides himself in and out of me. His fingertips dig into my hips, and it feels amazing despite the slight twinge of pain. It all mixes together perfectly.

Everything feels right: his hands, his mouth against mine, the way he's moving in and out of me—it all feels too good. My muscles tighten around him, and my head falls back, breaking our kiss. "Bennet," I call out, causing him to thrust deeper, harder.

As my release breaks and washes over me, his breathing speeds up. His body becomes hard, and his thrusts become more rapid and not as precise. Just as I begin floating down from my high, he removes himself from me and empties himself on to the shower floor. His head falls forward, resting against my shoulder as his breathing and heart rate calm.

Slowly, he places me on my feet, and we remove ourselves from one another. Neither of us talks as we gather our clothes and pull them back on. I wring my hair out over my shoulder and then toss the long mess behind me. I use the rubber band on my wrist to tie it back. I glance at myself in the mirror and see my mascara is running down my cheeks. I look like a drowned rat. I shake my head and wipe away the black from under my eyes.

When I have my clothes back on, even though they're wet, I pick up my shoes and hold them to my chest. "I guess I better get going," I say, motioning toward the door.

"Let me give you a ride," he says, grabbing his bag from his locker.

I look back toward the door, trying to come up with an excuse to just get out. "Thanks, but I'll just walk like I usually do."

He grabs my hand and stops me from walking out. "Maddie, you're soaking wet. You're going to freeze out there. Let me take you home."

My eyes fall to the floor, and I let out a deep breath. I offer up a small smile and nod. "Okay," I agree.

We walk back into the boxing room, and I grab my bag that I left on the floor. Then, he leads me out into the main gym and to the doors. He unlocks the glass doors and pushes them open. I walk through, and he quickly sets the alarm and steps out into the darkness with me. After he locks the door from the outside, he takes my hand in his and leads me to his car in the parking lot. I climb into my seat and stuff my bag between my feet. He takes his place behind the wheel and pushes the button to put the top up. Next, he turns on the heat. I don't even realize I'm shaking until I feel the warmth.

"Thank you," I say, cupping my hands together and catching the heat that's coming from the vents.

"You're welcome." He offers up a smile and shifts into gear.

We're only a couple blocks from my apartment when a firetruck comes rushing past us.

"Oh, wow. I wonder where that's going," I say, feeling my heart rate pick up at the startle it gave me.

"Looks like we're about to find out," Bennet says as the truck slows down and black smoke billows up ahead. He pulls over to maneuver past the truck and I see the source of the fire.

It's my building.

My mouth drops open, and my eyes grow wide, watching the flames licking the top of the building. Bennet pulls the car over as close as he can get to the building with the whole block being barricaded off.

He looks at me, the building, and back. "Oh my god! I'm sorry, Maddie."

I'm speechless. All I can do is nod my head.

———

BENNET WALKS me inside his house and into a guest room. He didn't give me a choice, really, just told me I'd be staying with him until I could get this nightmare sorted.

"You have a private bathroom through there," he says, pointing at one of the big, white doors. "I sent an email to my house manager; she'll be bringing by some clothes in your size. I'll be just across the hall if you need me."

He leaves me alone in the room without saying anything else.

I fall onto the bed and pull my phone from my bag.

"Hello?" Jazz answers.

"My building is on fire," I say, sounding a little off from still being in shock.

"What? Are you okay?"

I nod, forgetting that she can't see me.

"Mads, are you okay?" she asks again.

"Yeah, yeah, I'm fine. I wasn't there at the time. But everything is gone. The whole building was up in flames."

"I'm so sorry, honey. Do you need anything? You need a place to stay?"

"Yeah, I'll need a place to stay, but I'm fine for tonight. I was with a friend. I'll be over sometime tomorrow."

"Okay, if you need anything between now and then, call me. Okay, Mads?"

"Okay, thank you." Without another word, I hang up the phone and let it fall onto the bed beside me. I look around the room, feeling lost. I'm in a strange room, alone. Bennet isn't here next to me. I guess he's trying to give me a little space to wrap my head around this. But I don't want to be alone.

I stand and walk into the bathroom. It's big and fancy, but right now, I'm numb to it all. I step into the shower and wash off, wanting to scrub the last hour off my skin. When I get out, I walk back into the bedroom and open the dresser drawers. I don't know why because they're all empty. Habit, I guess. I look behind the bathroom door and grab the robe I spotted earlier. After brushing out my hair, I go in search of Bennet.

I knock on the door across from mine, and he pulls it open.

"I don't want to be alone," I admit.

He offers up a sad smile but steps to the side to allow me to come in.

He closes the door behind us. "How do a movie and junk food sound?"

I climb up onto his bed. "Sounds perfect."

"I'll be right back."

While he's gone, I lay back on his bed. His deep, rich scent engulfs me. Somehow, it settles my fears and worries. I'm nearly asleep when he walks in.

He sets the snacks down on the bench at the foot of the bed, "I didn't know what you'd want, so I just grabbed everything I could find."

I smile and rub my eyes awake as I pull the bag closer, peaking inside. I find chips, candy, and leftover Chinese takeout. I pick up the small white box. Opening it, I find orange chicken and fried rice. I grab one of the forks from inside the bag and take a bite. Even cold, it tastes delicious.

"I didn't take you for an orange chicken kind of guy."

"I'm not. It was ordered for me. I prefer something a little spicier."

He puts in the movie and crawls into bed next to me. He leans down, grabs two beers, and hands me one.

"Have you ever done this before?" I ask.

"What?"

"This. Got into bed with a girl just to eat crap and watch tv?"

He laughs. "No, not in a long time anyway. Maybe college."

I set my water down on the table and force my attention to the tv while I eat.

We eat, watch the movie, laugh, and talk. By the time the movie is ending, I'm lying next to him with his arm wrapped around me. The room going black makes me look over at him. "Is this too much?"

"What do you mean?"

"Well, we're both very insistent on not being in a relationship, but here we are, doing things people in relationships do."

"Just because we do things that people in relationships do doesn't mean we're in a relationship. I mean, people that are dating have dinner together, and we've done that."

"Good point." I hike my leg up over his hips.

"I like you, Maddie. I want you by my side, but I don't want you to feel you have to be. When we're together, we're together. When we're not, we're not. Sound easy enough?"

"Well, we're together now," I say, lifting and sliding myself onto his lap.

His hands move up to hold my hips. "We are," he agrees.

"Why don't you show me some more of those moves?"

Before I know it, he's rolling us over. His mouth lands on mine, and his hips grind against me. All it takes is two seconds before I've forgotten about everything but him. His hands roam my body freely, pushing and pulling my robe away. His mouth breaks away from mine, only to kiss and nibble his way down my body. It's like he knows all the right places to touch to have me quivering and whimpering, needing more.

His big hands massage my breasts, hips, and thighs. All the while, his mouth keeps going lower and lower. When his tongue runs between my folds, my hips buck upward like I've been struck by lightning. A sound escapes my lips, and it almost sounds foreign. This is not my first time, but for some reason, it feels like it is. Like every place he touches is a place that's never been touched before.

"Bennet," I call out his name in a whimper.

His hands on my hips squeeze tighter, his tongue moving quicker. My orgasm builds just beneath the surface, waiting for the exact right time to be set free. It causes my muscles to harden and tense. It halts my breathing in my chest; it makes me freeze until he flicks his tongue against me one last time. Finally, it shatters, washing over me. My toes curl while my fingers dig into the bed, fisting the sheets. I suck in a deep breath, and it leaves my lips in a rush as I call for him again and again.

When my body has gone completely limp, he pulls away and positions himself at my entrance.

"I have to be inside you, Maddie. Watching you come has me ready to explode," he says, pushing into me.

The second we become one, we both relax and let out a deep breath. He pauses his hips while his mouth finds mine, allowing my body to adjust to the intrusion. He kisses me soft and slow, and after a minute of kissing, his hips start moving again. He pushes into me further, slowly, rolls his hips and withdraws himself, only to do it all over again.

"Fuck, Maddie," he whispers, never stopping.

We spend the night in the same manner, never stopping. Only pausing until we start again. I don't fall asleep until the first bit of morning sun starts peeking through the windows.

———

IT FEELS like I've only been asleep for an hour when his alarm starts going off from beside the bed. I hear him groan and feel the mattress beneath me move just before it's silenced. He rolls back over, wrapping his arm around my stomach as he whispers in my ear, "Good morning, sleepyhead."

I smile from his breath tickling my cheek. "Ugh, I don't want to get up yet. I just went to sleep."

"What do you say we both call in? I mean, you have been through a traumatic experience."

With his words, all the panic and worry come rushing back into my head. "Fuck, I forgot about that."

He chuckles. "You forgot your apartment burned down?"

I nod. "Could you call my boss for me?" I laugh.

"I'll let Mr. Windsor know," he says, smacking my butt softly while crawling out of bed.

He leaves the room for a moment, then comes back. The smell of coffee perks me up.

He hands me a mug before planting a kiss on my forehead. "Give me a few moments. I'll be right back."

Twenty minutes later, I'm fighting off sleep when he walks back in the room.

"Breakfast in bed?" he asks, setting down a tray.

I sit up and find orange juice, eggs, toast, bacon, fresh fruit, and a bowl of whipped topping.

"Oh my god, Bennet, this is too much." I inhale the aroma and my stomach growls.

He picks up a strawberry and dips it into the whipped cream, feeding it to me. "Mr. Windsor said to take all the time you need. Your job will be safe."

I smile. "Mmmm, that's good," I practically moan around a mouth full.

He smiles. "I have an idea." He picks up a grape and pops it into his mouth while sitting down beside me.

"What's that?" I ask, picking up my coffee and taking a sip.

"After breakfast, I'll take you to the track and give you a ride."

"A ride in your race car?" My brows skyrocket.

He nods. "It's not NASCAR, but yeah. It's just a drag car."

"Yes! I'd love that." I put my coffee back down and pick up a strip of bacon. "I will need to get to Damon and Jazz's soon after though. I'm going to be staying there for a while."

His eyes grow wide. "About Damon..."

"What? What about Damon?"

"He's your brother?" he asks, as if seeking a confirmation.

I nod, realizing I hadn't given that detail a second thought until now.

"If you don't mind, can we not tell him what we're doing just yet? It's just that he's a pretty close friend, and I don't want him pissed at me for boning his sister."

I laugh. "We never have to tell him. It's none of his business who I'm boning," I say, using his term with a giggle.

"I think we should tell him at some point, but I think I should do it when the time is right."

I nod and shrug one shoulder. "Fine by me."

He picks up a fork and feeds me a bite of yolky egg. He smiles, and I feel my heart pick up as excitement races through my veins.

8

BENNET

We have breakfast in bed, and she goes back to her room to find something to wear that Quinn picked out while I shower and dress. I wash off quickly so that I don't hold us up, then pull on a pair of jeans and a t-shirt. As I'm stepping out of my bedroom, she's walking out of hers. I look her up and down with a grin.

"What's that?" I ask, motioning toward a pressed pants suit.

She laughs. "All the clothes in that closet are dress clothes. Not one single pair of jeans. I appreciate the high end labels your house manager picked out, but maybe she could have chosen something casual." She flaps the jacket lapels as she speaks.

"Come on," I say, stepping past her and opening the dresser. "In this house, jeans are not hung up because they're not appropriate, according to my mother. Quinn, my house manager, was handpicked and trained by my mother, so I'm guessing she drilled that into her like she did me as a child."

She scrunches up her face. "Your mom set up your house?"

I laugh and nod. "Yeah, I was too busy to do it." I start stepping back toward the door. "T-shirts are also in the drawers. I'll be downstairs." I close the door behind me and head into the kitchen, where I grab a bottle of water from the fridge.

"Good morning, Quinn," I say, tipping the bottle upward and taking a drink.

"Good morning, sir." She looks me up and down. "Don't you look nice. No work today?"

I shake my head. "Not today. Today, I have company."

She nods as her eyes narrow. "I must meet the woman who's gotten under your skin enough to make you call off work. She must be something else." She shoots me a grin.

I can't help but smile. "That she is," I agree.

The door swings open and in walks Maddie. She's wearing a tight pair of jeans and a shirt that ends just above her bellybutton. Her long, dark hair is hanging around her in soft waves, a look many women go out of their way to get, and her hair does it all on its own.

I reach for her. "Maddie, this is my manager, Quinn. Quinn, this is a friend from work, Maddie."

They both smile and shake hands.

"The jeans look great on you; looks like Bennet's assessment of your size was spot on." I can sense the underhandedness in Quinn's comment, and I'm not about to engage with her any further.

"Well, now that that's out of the way, we really should get going." I step toward the door that leads to the garage. Opening it, I hold it open for Maddie as she walks through.

We climb into the Mercedes, and I take down the top since it's a nice warm day. I back out of the garage and zoom down the driveway, pausing at the gate until it opens. She pulls out a pair of sunglasses and puts them on, hiding her beautiful eyes from the sun. As I drive down the freeway with the wind in our hair, I can't keep my eyes off her. Everything about her is beautiful: the way her hair blows around her, wild and free; the way the sun kisses her ivory skin, making it sparkle and light up; and way her lips turn up in the corners, never actually smiling, but revealing enough to let me know she's already having a good time.

Just being with her, watching her, it put something back into my life I haven't felt in a long time: excitement, purpose. I've just been going through the motions. I go to work and do my job, never really feeling important or needed. I go to the gym where I can work out every bit of anger and frustration I've felt through the day from being forced to be someone I'm not. And then, at night, I find a random girl to bring home to distract myself from how lonely I truly am.

Maddie, she changes all of that. At work, I get excited about running into her. Seeing how excited she gets over something as simple as numbers, it makes me want to work harder for her. I now have fun at the gym; forgetting all about the shitty parts of work, I can just be with her. And at night—well, last night anyway—I have her. And there's no way I'm letting her walk away easily. Even if she comes to me and says, "I want more." I'll bend over backward to give her everything she asks for. I realize how out of character this is for me, and on the surface, that scares me. But deep down, something keeps telling me it's right—that I shouldn't worry because everything is as it should be.

It's not long before we're pulling into the track. The owner, an old friend, Dave, steps out of a storage building when he sees us pull in. He comes walking over just as we're climbing out.

"How's it been, Bennet?" he asks, holding out his hand to shake.

I smile and shake his hand. "Good, and yourself?" I ask.

He nods. "As good as ever, I guess. Who's this beauty?" He motions toward Maddie.

I pull her to my side. "This is Maddie," I answer, letting it drop there because I'm not quite sure what to call her. Earlier I called her my friend from work, and while she didn't say anything, I saw a flash of something on her face.

"You bring her out here to see how fast you can drive?" he jokes.

I laugh. "I did. You mind if I get the car out?"

He shakes his head. "Not at all. I'll even run the board for ya." He pulls his red hat out of his back pocket and slaps it on his head, covering his gray hair. "Come with me, little lady. I'll give you the best seat in the house," he tells her.

"I beg to differ. The best seat in the house is right next to me." I laugh as he takes her arm and leads her away.

I walk into the garage and down the rows of cars until I find mine. I unlock the container it's held in. Racing is a big game. You don't want to leave your car sitting around for anyone to fuck with. So, many of us leave them here at the track. We pay a pretty penny to do so, but it's a lot easier than loading them up on a flatbed every time we want to race.

I walk into the small garage it's been locked up in and slide behind the wheel. I twist the key that's already in the ignition and the car roars to life. I rev the engine a few times to get her warmed up before shifting into gear and hitting the gas. I drive around the track and to the starting line. Again, I rev the engine to let Dave know I'm ready. The lights change: 3…2…1. And I shift into first gear and hit the gas. My car goes soaring forward, barreling down the track. My heart is pounding with excitement and adrenaline. All I can think about is crossing that finish line, and hoping I have a good time to impress Maddie. I know she says she's not impressed by material things, but this isn't something you can buy. This is pure talent, dedication, and years of hard work.

When I circle back around, she comes running out of the stands. Her face shows pure happiness and excitement. I shut off the car and get out, catching her as she runs into my arms.

"That was amazing!" she cheers me on.

I laugh.

Dave steps out too. "That wasn't shit. Seven-point-eight seconds?" He laughs.

"Hey, it was my first run. Let the car get warmed up some," I tell him, placing Maddie on her feet.

"Don't listen to him, babe. You were awesome."

Hearing her call me babe makes me freeze, but I shake it off quickly, hopeful she didn't notice.

"You think that's amazing, you need to come down on a Saturday night. That's when you'll see amazing." Dave's smiling from ear to ear.

He lives for the races, which is why he started this place up over thirty years ago.

"Can we?" Maddie asks, turning to me.

I nod. "Sure, I don't see why not," I agree.

―――――

WHEN WE GET BACK to my place, Maddie insists on getting over to Damon's. I hate to see her go, but I don't want to be the clingy type. She grabs the things she had with her at the gym and asks if my driver can take her over in the town car since we don't want Damon to see her getting out of my car.

We load up in the back, and my driver climbs behind the wheel. As we drive across town, I hold her hand between us.

"I had a lot of fun today. Thank you for helping take my mind off of everything." She offers a sweet smile.

"Come here," I whisper, leaning in for a kiss.

She leans over and catches my lips with hers. I place my hand on her jaw and hold her to me as I deepen the kiss.

"I'm going to miss you in my bed tonight," I whisper against her lips.

Her blue eyes seem to darken. "I'm going to miss being in your bed." She begins kissing me again.

I pull away. "Are you sure you want to go to your brother's?" I ask with a grin, hoping it seduces her into coming back home with me.

"I'm sure. We have our arrangement, and I'm afraid staying over every night will complicate that."

I nod in agreement, even though it wouldn't bother me to complicate things a bit. Thinking that scares me, and I quickly change gears. Any other woman and I'd be dying to get rid of her at this point. Why is she different? Why am I so willing to throw away all my beliefs all for one girl?

"Here we are, ma'am," the driver says.

She leans over and presses a kiss to my mouth so quick that I don't have time to respond. "I'll talk to you later," she says, opening her door and running toward the house.

The driver doesn't wait for her to get inside, he just drives away the second the door is shut. I don't ask him to stay. I don't say anything. I'm confused by the thoughts swirling around my head. On the one hand, I'm terrified of her wanting more, of having to come up with a bullshit compromise that will keep her in my life and probably hurt her. I also can't stomach the thought of letting her walk away if things get to be too complicated.

When I get home, the house is quiet—the way I usually like it—but now, it feels too quiet, too lonely. I head to my study and pour a glass of scotch, then sit at my desk and look around the room. I don't ever remember being bored before. What did I do before? I entertained myself with the gym, booze, and women. But suddenly, finding women has no appeal.

I'm lost in thought when Quinn walks into the room. "Mr. Windsor, is there anything I can do for you?" she asks, slowly walking closer.

I wave my hand in the air. "I'm fine, thanks."

She steps in front of me. "Are you sure? You seem lonely, sad. I can cheer you up," she offers, raising her hands and unbuttoning her top. Before I can move to stop her or say anything, her top is open, and her bare breasts are there, right before my eyes. They're big and round and perky. Obviously fake, but perfect, nonetheless.

"I'd love to make you feel better, Mr. Windsor," she says, walking closer, rubbing her hands over them and making them bounce.

I tip back the rest of the glass and stand, my eyes never leaving her. She thinks I'm falling for her trap as I close the distance between us. I grab her shirt on either side of her body and pull it together. "You're fired, Quinn. Please leave immediately, and don't forget to call my mother for your last week's pay."

She nods slowly, and her eyes fall to the ground as she spins around.

"And if she asks why you were fired, I wouldn't lie. Because I sure as hell won't," I add on, picking up my glass and refilling it.

———

I'M SITTING in the study, alone, watching the fire as I drink my third glass of scotch. My phone rings from in my pocket, and I pull it out.

"Hello?" I answer.

"Hey, Bennet," Damon says. "I got an unexpected house guest, and they're having a bit of a girls' night tonight. Want to get out for a while, have a few drinks?"

I look at my watch to see that it's only eight o'clock. "Yeah, why not? Did you have a place in mind?"

"Maury's Pub?"

"Alright, I'll be there in twenty."

Since I've already had too much to drink, I grab an Uber, I'll give my driver the night off. Damon is already there, sitting in a small booth in the back corner by himself. I stop at the bar, grab a beer, and head over.

"What's up, man?" I ask, sliding into the booth.

He shakes his head as he picks up his beer, taking a sip. "Not much. What have you been doing?"

I do the same, not sure what to say since what I'm doing is his baby sister.

"Man, I got my sister at the house right now. Her place burned down. It's like being a kid and getting picked on all over again."

I laugh but pull my brows together, confused.

"Jazz has always been my sister's best friend. We all grew up together. So, I've been through so many of these sleepovers, I can't even keep count anymore."

I nod, understanding. "That sucks about your sister's place. I hope she had insurance."

He nods. "She did, but it will take some time for the check to come in. And then she'll have the whole process of finding a new place." He lets out a deep breath as his eyes grow wide. "God, I dread it. It took her months to decide on the place she had. And if I know her, she'll probably end up bunking with that worthless boyfriend of hers."

"Boyfriend?" I ask, a knot forming in my stomach.

"Yeah, when Jazz and I were getting together, she introduced us to this loser, Travis I think was his name. I thought they broke it off, but she stayed somewhere last night and wouldn't say where. They're probably back together."

I nod as my worries fade, realizing Travis is her cover. "Why don't you like him?" I ask, just to make chitchat.

"He's just a loser. He's this skinny punk kid that wears baggy pants, has gold chains, and tattoos all over the place, such a fucking poser. He's just the kind of guy you know will never get any kind of decent job. Would you want your sister with that?"

I laugh, but I can't imagine hanging out with the kind of guy Damon's describing. "My sister is basically the same. She graduated with a degree in art." I snort. "I mean, I get doing what you love, but sometimes what you love doesn't pay the bills. Which is why she's in the position she's in now. She called me a sellout because I took over the company to make money and keep our parents off my back. I mean, I still do the things I like on my downtime."

"You still race?" he asks.

"Not as much, but when I feel like it."

"What about boxing?" he asks, and with that question, he has a moment of clarity. His face goes slack, and his eyes glaze over like he's remembering something. Then, his eyes find mine, and they narrow in anger.

9

MADDIE

When Bennet drops me off, I rush into the house before Jazz and Damon notice a strange car in front of their house.

I let myself in. "Hello? Honey, I'm home," I joke, walking through the foyer and finding them in the living room, sitting on the couch and watching tv.

Jazz smiles when she sees me. "'Bout time you got here. I've been waiting all day," she says.

I flop down on the couch between them, just to be annoying. "This is going to be just like old times! We can pick on Damon. Only this time, Mom isn't here for him to run to." I laugh, and so does Jazz. When we look over at Damon, he doesn't look impressed.

"Is that what we're doing tonight? Having a slumber party?" He arches an eyebrow.

I look over at Jazz, and she looks at me.

"Just for tonight; tomorrow night and every other will be business as usual. I promise," Jazz says, smiling sweetly at him to get her way.

"Alright. I'll get out of here and let you have your naked pillow fights and do makeovers."

My face pinches. "You know that's not what happens at slumber parties, right?"

He groans. "See, you've been here for five minutes, and already you're ruining my dreams. Actually fuck that, the fact you're my sister ruined it." He swipes the keys off the table. As he heads for the door, he bends over the back of the couch, giving Jazz a goodbye kiss.

"Hey you're the one that brought it up sicko!" I shout after him.

The moment I hear the door close behind him, I turn to Jazz. "I know you're pregnant, but what liquor do you have up in here. I'm stressed as hell."

She offers up a smile. "I bet you are. I'd be freaking out if I lost all my stuff."

We stand, and she leads me into the kitchen.

"Did you guys get all your stuff from your old apartment?" I ask.

She nods as she digs me out a beer. "Yeah, we picked it up and took most of it directly to the country house."

I snort. "The country house?"

She laughs. "That's what we're calling it. This," she motions around the house we're in, the house in the city, "is the townhouse."

I laugh. "I don't think that's what townhouse means."

She jerks her head toward me. "What do you mean?"

"Townhouses are those houses that are built side by side, like they have a front yard and a back yard, but no side yard because it's built onto another house. It's not a townhouse because it's in town."

She laughs. "Really?"

I nod and take a drink of my beer. "You really thought it meant that?"

She nods and laughs so hard, she snorts.

"Damon didn't tell you?"

She's now sitting on the floor, laughing and shaking her head.

I can't help but join in on her laughter. "That's funny. He probably thinks it's cute that you think that."

Her laughter dies down, and she wipes the tears from her eyes. Holding out her hand, I pull her back up.

She pops some popcorn, and we head back into the living room. "So, tell me about the new guy you're seeing."

"How do you know I'm seeing a new guy?" I ask, taking a big swig of beer.

"Come on, Mads." She levels her eyes on me. "We've known one another for, like, our whole lives. You think I don't know when you're getting some? Spill it." She grabs my knee and shakes it.

I laugh and roll my eyes. "I am seeing someone, but you can't tell Damon."

"Is it Bennet? It's Bennet, isn't it?"

I try not to smile, but I do as I shake my head. "We're not together-together, though."

She cuts her eyes to me. "What does that mean?"

"It means, we're hanging out, we're hooking up, but there's no attachment. No strings. No nothing. When we're together, we're together. When we're not, we're not. That easy."

She laughs. "Yeah, okay."

"What?" I ask.

"That literally never works out, Mads. Have you not seen a movie in the last twenty years?"

"Do you not know me? All of my relationships are strictly friends with benefits."

"Yeah because you pick duds that you get bored with after a few weeks. This one will be different. This one will either last forever, or it will break you forever."

My mouth drops open. "What a mean thing to say!" I gently smack her leg, not trying to hurt the pregnant lady.

She shrugs. "It's just how I see it."

I shake my head. "No. No way. Bennet and I are two in the same. He doesn't do love, and I don't either. I'm keeping my distance. No way am I going to fall in love with Bennet Windsor."

She snorts. "But is he keeping his distance? He's clearly already invited you to stay the night. Did you sleep in the same bed? Did you spend the day together?"

"Yes and yes, but what does that have to do with anything?"

She turns herself so that she's facing me instead of the tv. "How many hook-ups have you had?"

I shrug.

"Okay, well how many hook-ups have you had that lead to staying the night, sleeping together, and spending the whole next day together? Not to mention you work out together and work together."

I look at her while I think.

Zero.

I mean, some have had many of those things, but not all. Never all. I didn't stay the whole night with anyone until Travis. And even then, I never stayed the whole next day with him. If anything, it was a miracle even to have breakfast together.

Oh fuck. What if she's right? What if Bennet is getting too close without even realizing it? This is definitely something I need to talk to him about.

"See, I told you," Jazz says, fixing her eyes back on the tv but keeping the small grin on her face.

I sit back and drink my beer, thinking over everything she's said. What would happen if Bennet and I got serious? Would we get married? Would I move into that big, fancy mansion of his? Would we have kids? I don't want any of that. I don't want to tie myself to another human being. I don't want to bring kids into this world. Who wants to pass on this shitty existence to another person? And that mansion, don't get me started. I'd much prefer a reasonably sized home that wouldn't require a staff to clean.

"What in the hell are you thinking about so hard over there?" she asks, cutting through my thoughts.

"Moving to the country and living off the land," I confess.

She laughs long and hard. "Okay, that's not you. Where's that coming from?"

I shrug. "I'm just tired. I'm tired of people and their standards. I'm tired of working as hard as I do and still struggling."

"Whoa, didn't you get a raise with that new job?"

I nod. "I did, but still. I'm working myself to death every day just to live. I mean, I can't afford a real vacation. I can't travel the world. Have you ever thought about how much money you spend at the store just to eat, and then you gotta spend more money on toilet paper! Vicious cycle," I rant.

She takes my beer from my hands and places it on the table. She then stands and grabs my wrist, pulling me up.

"What are you doing?" I ask.

She takes me to the bathroom. "You're seriously overstressed. I mean, did you listen to what you just said? Who thinks that? Take a long hot bath. There's bath oil, bombs, and bubbles, everything you could possibly need. Light the candles. Play some soft music. Just unwind. Then, go to bed because I think you're delirious. But Maddie, don't let all the shit I just mentioned freak you out. If you think you have control of the situation with Bennet and you've both agreed to the terms...what do I know?"

I laugh and shake my head. "You're probably right. I didn't get much sleep last night," I confess.

She smiles wide and nods her head. "I bet. Mr. Boxer got all up in that, huh?"

I laugh and shake my head. "What? No. Get out!" I point toward the door, and she slips out, laughing the whole way.

I bend down and run the water for a bath. I dump in some fancy bubbles, and while the tub fills, I light the candles. Finally, I strip down and turn off the lights. As I slide deep into the tub, I pull up some music on my phone and set it on top of the toilet lid. I close my eyes and lean back, letting the scent of lavender and eucalyptus ease my worries away. I take a deep breath and feel like I'm exhaling all negative things away. My neck is sore and stiff, but the hot water helps to break up the tension. Before I know it, I'm fast asleep... until my phone rings. I jump awake and answer it quickly.

"Hello?" I answer.

"He knows," Bennet says on the other end of the line.

"Who knows what? What are you talking about?"

"Your brother, he knows about us."

I sit up quickly, causing the water to splash over the side of the tub. "How?"

"He invited me out for some drinks. We started talking about things. He told me about you coming to stay, then asked if I still raced. Then he asked if I still boxed, and then he put two and two together. He said you mentioned getting hit on by a hot boxer."

"Fuck," I whisper. "How'd he take it?"

"I'm not sure. He didn't say anything else. He just stood up and left. So, expect him to come in hot."

"Great," I mumble. "Thanks for the warning."

"Will I see you tomorrow?" he asks quietly, like he's afraid I'll say no.

"I don't even know if I'll be alive tomorrow." Without another word, I hang up the phone and stand from the tub. I wrap a towel around myself and hit the drain. I flip on the light and start blowing out the candles when I hear a door slam.

"Where is she?" he asks Jazz.

"She's taking a bath. What's wrong?" she asks, quietly but also urgently.

He doesn't answer.

I quickly open the door and step out into the hallway, nearly bumping into him.

"Bennet? Really?" His chest is rising and falling quickly. The vein in his neck is popping out, and his jaw is cocked. I don't know if I've ever seen him this mad.

"Damon," I start, but he cuts me off.

"No, Madeline. For the first time in your life, just tell me the truth. Are you sleeping with Bennet?"

"I don't think this is any of our business," Jazz tries, but he doesn't budge.

He stares me down, and I stare him down. Jazz stands off to the side, bouncing from one foot to the other, eyes flashing back and forth between us.

Finally, I take a deep breath. "Yes," I admit.

He shakes his head and turns to walk away, but I follow after him.

"What's the problem with Bennet? Huh?" I ask, following him into the kitchen.

He swings the refrigerator door open and snatches a beer. He twists the top open, tosses the cap in the trash, and takes a long drink.

"Didn't you say many times that you wish I'd stop messing around with all these fuckboys and find someone that has a decent job, that's a decent guy?"

He refuses to look at me.

"That's what I thought, Damon." I turn to leave, but stop myself, remembering I have no place to go. "You're my brother, Damon. Not my dad. And I didn't see you rushing to tell me when you started fucking my best friend, did you?"

"Is that why you're doing this? To get back at me?" he asks, holding his arms out at his sides, cold green eyes locked on mine.

"What? No. No, I'm not trying to get back at you. I love that you two are together. I love that you both found someone equally great. I'm happy that you're getting married and having a baby. I love that you two get your happily ever after. But why am I being treated like your fucked-up little sister when I try to do the same?" Without another word, I walk back down the hall and into the bathroom, slamming the door behind me. I sit on the edge of the tub, and a deep breath escapes me. Tears fill my eyes, not because I'm hurt or sad, but because I'm angry. He's my brother, and he's Bennet's friend. He should be happy that I'm with such a decent guy instead of Travis.

I hear a soft knock on the door and I dry my eyes. Jazz walks in holding a pair of clothes. "I knew you didn't have anything, so I brought you some P.J.'s."

I take them. "Thank you."

She nods. "Just give him some time. Remember how mad you were when you found out about us? He'll come around, Mads. We're going to bed, so the couch is all yours."

I don't look up until I hear the click of the door closing behind her.

I stand and pull on the clothes that she brought me while thinking about everything all over again: Bennet, Damon, what Jazz just said. I don't see why I'm fighting so hard for something that doesn't even really exist. I could end things with Bennet if I want to. But I don't feel that I should. Damon doesn't have the right to say who I can and can't date—er… sleep with rather. I didn't demand he stop seeing Jazz, and I hope he allows me the same opportunity. I know how I am. If you tell me no, I'll want it that much more. If Damon tells me to end it with Bennet, I'll fucking marry him to prove a point.

God, I hope I don't end up married. I shake my head at myself.

I head to the couch in the dark house. Flopping onto the soft cushions, I pull the blanket up around me. For a second, I feel lonely and wish I would've stayed with Bennet, but that thought alone brings on a whole new fear, and I push it away just like everything else. I focus on how comfortable I am. I listen to the soft hum of the A/C unit when it's on, and I count down the minutes until it starts back up. I look up at the blinds and watch as bits of dust dance around in the shine of the streetlights, almost like glitter. I focus on my heartbeat, wishing it were faster like it was last night when I was with him. A sigh leaves my lips. Is it Bennet I miss or his company? Is it the things he says, or is it the way he touches me and makes me feel alive? It's all of it, I finally admit to myself.

I pick up my phone from the coffee table and debate on whether or not I should call him. Then see that it's pushing midnight and figure I better not. I drop it back onto the table and curl myself into a ball. It seems like it takes forever, but I finally fall asleep.

10

BENNET

"You. You're the boxer," Damon says, narrowing his eyes at me. My mouth opens, but no sound comes out. I can't deny it, but I don't want to admit it either.

He shakes his head, then pushes his way out of the booth, heading for the door. I stand up and watch him go, unsure of what I should do. He climbs behind the wheel of his Jeep and squeals the tires off the pavement as he leaves.

I sit back down and pull out my phone, calling Maddie.

After we talk, it feels like things are just a bigger mess than they were already. She wouldn't give me an answer about seeing her tomorrow either. I tell myself that I'm overthinking, that I've just had too much to drink and need to sleep it off.

I stand and head back out to the parking lot. Crawling into the backseat, the driver asks where I want to go next. I quickly think it over, debating between my usual club or the house. A part of me wants to go have a few more drinks, maybe find someone to take home, but Maddie flashes into my head, and all I can say is, "Take me home."

That reply only makes me think more. Maddie and I, we have an agreement. And nowhere in that agreement did it say we can't sleep with other people. But I don't want to sleep with other people. I just want her. How the hell did she get under my skin so quickly?

When we pull up to the house, I stumble my way in and up the stairs, falling into bed still completely dressed. It only takes seconds before I'm fast asleep.

————

MY PHONE RINGING pulls me from my dreams. I wiggle around until I can slide my hand in my pocket and pull it free.

"Hello?" I answer, still half asleep.

"Mr. Windsor, this is Nathan, your front gate guard. There is a Madeline Strickland trying to get in. Should I let her in or call the police?"

"Let her in," I nearly yell. "Always let her in."

"Yes, sir."

I drop the phone onto the bed and stretch. Finally, I sit up and tug off my shoes.

Maddie walks in, a smirk on her face. "Did someone have a late night?"

I nod. "Late, drunk, whatever," I mumble.

She crawls up onto the bed with me, pushing me back down. She holds her head up by one fist while her leg drapes over my hips.

"How'd it go with Damon?" I ask, rubbing my head.

"He had a fit. But today, when they got up for work, he didn't say anything."

"Fuck, work," I mumble. "I should go in."

"Or, you could hang out with me all day. You seem pretty hungover."

"Thirty-year-old scotch will do that to you."

She giggles, and it's like music to my ears. "I'd love to, but I need to go in. And you need to go shopping for your formal dress for this gala," I say, moving her leg off of me and attempting to stand.

"I can't afford a new dress, Bennet. My apartment just burned down." She sits up, one leg hanging over the edge of the bed.

I place my hand on her cheek, causing her to look up at me. "There's a list of stores that I have an account with. I'll give you the info, and you can go get a dress, shoes, jewelry, anything you want without having to pay a dime."

"No, I can't do that; it feels like you're my sugar daddy," she argues, shaking her head.

I sit on the bed and roll us so that I'm on top, even though it makes my head spin. "You already agreed to go with me. Are you going to stand me up now?"

Her cheeks turn the slightest shade of pink. "Well, no."

"Alright, then go shopping." I press a kiss to her mouth before pulling away and standing. I can feel her eyes on me as I walk into the connected bathroom for my morning shower.

I'm standing under the flow of hot water, eyes closed while it pours down over my head. I feel a cold draft hit my back, then warm arms wrap around my stomach. I spin around and find Maddie, smiling up at me.

I let out a chuckle as I pull her lips to mine. Picking her up, she wraps her legs around my hips, and I press her back to the wall. My mouth devours hers, while my right hand rubs over her sensitive clit. I slide a finger inside, and she lets out a deep moan. That sound is like taking a lightning bolt to the dick. It jumps alive, pressing against her like it knows where it wants to be. Taking myself in hand, I place it at her entrance and push forward until we're connected.

"I don't want anyone but you, Maddie," I whisper against her lips as I move my hips back and then forward again. "You're different. You're so goddamn beautiful and sexy. Smart and talented. Kind and sweet," I say, pumping in and out of her with every word.

Her eyes open and lock on mine. All I can see is blue, like I'm looking into the deepest ocean. Her plump lips part with her heavy breathing and her nails dig into my biceps.

"Bennet," she says in a hushed whisper.

"Maddie," I reply, moving my lips back to hers. I kiss her deeply while never stilling my hips. I keep going, keep pushing her to feel me, to love me. I've never needed love from any woman, but with her, it's all I want. I want her to love me. I want her by my side for the rest of my life. And if she wants marriage and kids, I'll be more than willing to give her that. I'll give her anything she asks for as long as I have her.

As my release rises to the surface, she begins moaning against my lips. Her muscles are squeezing my dick, making it extremely hard not to come this very second. Finally, when I feel her relax around me and her moans have quieted, I let go, riding out the waves of my orgasm and emptying myself onto the shower floor.

———

I HAVE a smile as I walk into the office today, something I don't usually have. Being with Maddie makes me happy. And it's not just because we had sex. Just being with her, holding her hand, talking, lying next to her, it genuinely makes me happy. I'm still a little confused as to why I feel this way around her when it's never happened with any other woman, but I'm trying not to overthink it. I tell myself just to enjoy it while it lasts.

When I step into my office, I find Callan at my drink cart. He's standing near the window looking out over the city.

"You're here early," I say, going straight to my desk and setting down my briefcase.

He spins around. "What did you find out about the assistant?" he asks.

"I'm sorry, man. I completely forgot," I tell him. "I'll call her now."

"Who do you have in mind?" He sits in the empty chair across the desk from mine.

"My sister."

His eyebrows skyrocket. "Val?"

I nod.

"Doesn't she have a job?"

I laugh. "She has a hobby, and you know as well as I do that hobbies don't pay bills. She's been borrowing money off me every month for her rent. She needs a job, even if she doesn't want to admit it."

"Alright, well, just let me know what you find out," he says, standing and moving toward the doors.

"If I were you, I'd start looking through the applications. It's going to take some talking to get her to agree."

He laughs and nods, but walks out, leaving me alone.

I pick up the phone and dial her number.

"Hello?" she answers.

"Little sister, what have you been up to?"

"Why are you calling, Bennet? We both know you don't call unless you want something."

"I guess that's mutual then, isn't it?"

I can practically hear her eyes roll.

"How's the art thing coming along?"

"Why? You asking to rub it in my face?"

"No, I really want to know. Is business picking up?"

"No," she confesses. "I wish it were, but I've been thinking about what you said."

"What I said?" I ask, shocked.

"Yeah, you know, about getting a job and doing my art as a hobby."

"That's great, Val. That's why I'm calling."

"Oh?"

"Callan has a spot open for an assistant. It's five days a week, eight hours a day, and you get full benefits. That would give you the money you need to pay your bills, and you'll be able to see a real doctor when you need one instead of going to that crazy quack down the road for her herbal concoctions."

She snorts. "You are a snob; you know that?"

I open my mouth to snap back but decide against it.

"This is my life, Bennet. I know you and Mom and Dad don't understand it, but it's not your job to understand. It's your job to be supportive." Without another word, she hangs up the phone.

I shake my head and set the phone down, not at all surprised with how the conversation turned out. I'll give her some time. The next time she calls asking for money, I'm going to turn her down, though. If she's not willing to help herself, I'm not going to keep supporting her behavior. There's nothing wrong with chasing after a dream, but when you start losing things, it's time to get serious.

I turn on the computer and start going through the massive amounts of emails and phone messages. I begin replying to them when my phone rings.

"Hello?"

"They won't let me have the dress," Maddie says.

"What?"

"They say I'm not authorized on your account."

"Okay, send me the location, and I'll be down in a few," I tell her, rushing to finish the email I'm writing. When my phone chimes with a text message, I pick it up and leave the office.

It takes me a good twenty minutes to make it there with traffic, but I quickly park and walk into the store.

"Mr. Windsor," a staff member greets me.

I walk past and give a nod hello, heading straight to the counter where I see Maddie standing, looking embarrassed. Her arms are crossed over her chest, and her eyes are narrowed.

"Mr. Windsor," Meredith greets me. She's known my family for close to two decades.

"What's going on, Meredith?" I ask, motioning toward Maddie.

"I'm sorry, sir, but we can't let just anyone charge things to your account."

"You think this woman just picked a random store and knew I had a charge account here?"

"Well, no. But...I understand your frustration, sir. It's for your protection," she insists.

I laugh and glance over again at Maddie, feeling embarrassed for her. I feel like I'm walking on eggshells, constantly fearful that any little thing like this will scare her away.

"Have you rung the item up?" I ask.

She nods.

"Good, thank you, Meredith. In the future, I trust this won't be an issue?" She gives me a curt smile and wishes us a good day as we walk out of the store.

I look over nervously at Maddie, who hasn't said a word. "Hey, I'm sorry about that. I—"

"How dare she *Pretty Woman* me!"

I burst into laughter, not expecting that response.

"I ought to go back in there tomorrow and buy everything I want." She crosses her arms over her chest. "Big mistake. HUGE!" she says, reenacting the famous Julia Roberts scene.

"You can. You should," I agree, knowing that she doesn't have any clothes of her own.

"No, I can't. I can't afford it, and I don't want your money. I meant what I said earlier. I don't want this turning into some weird sugar daddy shit, or even worse, prostitution."

I reach out and take her hand in mine. "It's just money, Maddie. I have plenty, and I'll make more tomorrow. I know you can use it more than I can. Might as well spoil yourself a little."

"I don't wear that kind of shit, Bennet. I'm just fine going to the mall and buying a pair of jeans that cost twenty bucks. I don't need name brands and labels."

"Alright," I agree, driving her back to my house. It's evident she has a chip on her shoulder about being independent and providing for herself.

I carry her bags up to my bedroom as she throws herself onto my bed. I lay down beside her. "So, how was your night with your brother and soon-to-be sister-in-law."

"It kind of sucked. I had to sleep on the couch, and now my back is killing me. I wish that check would come in the mail so I could find a new place."

"Why don't you stay here?" I ask, rubbing her back. "I have plenty of room. You can stay in the room across the hall, or you could stay here with me."

She rolls to her side so she can look up at me. "Wouldn't that complicate things?"

I frown.

"I mean, neither of us wants a relationship. If we're sleeping together every night, won't that be like we're dating and living together?"

"Maddie, it's a relationship. That doesn't mean we are getting married or that we are chained to each other but don't bury your head in the sand. I'm not putting any rules on you. You can come and go as you please and truthfully…" I hesitate, questioning if I want to say the next part. "Truthfully, you can still date whoever you want."

"So what are we then?"

I shake my hand. "I'm not doing the label thing. I have the room that your brother doesn't. If you want it, take it. We'll deal with anything else that comes up later."

She smiles at me. "Okay, thank you." She grabs me by my shirt and pulls me down, pressing her lips to mine.

I feel my body relax with relief, hoping we both aren't just kidding ourselves with this situation.

MADDIE

"I should probably get back to work soon," I tell Bennet as we lay in bed with one another, not doing anything but holding each other while talking.

"There's no rush. Brian is there, so the job is still getting done. And your manager knows your situation. Your job will be safe when you come back," he says, absentmindedly running his hands through my hair.

"I know, but I need some normalcy. This bouncing from place to place and spending my days doing nothing is going to kill me." I turn my head so I can look back up at him. "Do you have to go back today?"

"Yeah, I'm going back after lunch. But you could use this time to pamper yourself for Friday night."

"What do you mean?"

"Go get your hair done. Get a mani/pedi. Get a massage. Let me spoil you a little."

"I don't know," I say, feeling a little nervous. "That's too much. You've done so much for me already."

He rolls us over, pinning me beneath him. "Damnit, Maddie. This, the buying you things and paying for stuff, it doesn't mean anything to me beyond spending money on someone I care about. There's no underhanded weird shit going on. Can't you see that?"

I nod. "Yes, but it does mean something to me. I owe you enough already."

"You don't owe me a fucking thing." He leans in and closes the distance between us, pressing his soft lips to mine. I close my eyes and let his kiss sink in. It warms me up from the inside out. It causes a tingle to swirl around in the pit of my stomach. It steals the air from my lungs and makes my muscles tighten with anticipation. How can one kiss do this?

He breaks the kiss and stands up, pulling me up with him. "Let's get some lunch. Then I'm going to go back to work, and I'll have Sarah make you those appointments."

I groan. "You're not going to give up on this, are you?"

He laughs. "Not a chance."

"I can make my own damn appointments!" I shout, playfully tossing a pillow at him as he walks towards the bathroom.

––––––

IT'S GOING on eight o'clock, and already I've had my hair deep conditioned, trimmed, and blown out. My nails are a soft ballet pink, and my toes match perfectly. I've gotten a spray tan and a massage. You'd think all this pampering would relax me and make me feel rested, but it's quite exhausting. The whole time I wonder how I'm going to repay him. I wonder why he's doing these things for me, even when I resist. I start to worry that he is getting too close. But then, I realize that all this may be entirely normal for him. I mean, I don't know if he does these things with the other women he's been with. He has money, and he likes to spend it. I shouldn't be making such a deal out of it. Just because it's big to me doesn't mean it's big to him. It's not like he's offering to buy me a car or new apartment. I need to trust what he said about it earlier.

I let out a sigh and force the worry in my head to drift away with it. The driver pulls through the gate of the house.

I let myself inside and find Bennet moving around the kitchen.

"Are you cooking?" I ask.

He nods. "I thought I'd show you I'm a man of many talents." He winks, "So, dinner is on me tonight." He spins around, and his eyes lock on mine.

"You look…" His sentence drifts off.

"Tan?" I ask, looking down at myself.

"I was going to say amazing, but yeah."

I hold up my hands, showing him my nails. "And I have these daggers stuck to my fingers."

He laughs but pulls me in for a kiss. "You look beautiful," he says, stepping away.

"It's going to take some getting used to. What are you cooking?" I lean against the island.

"You'll see. Why don't you go relax on the couch, and I'll get you when it's done?"

My phone rings and I pull it out of my back pocket to see Damon's name on the screen.

"Hello?" I answer, walking out of the kitchen and up the stairs.

"Where are you?" he asks.

"Why? Feel like yelling at me some more?"

He lets out a long breath. "Maddie, I was caught off guard."

"And?"

"And I never should have yelled at you. I just freaked out because, well, because I know Bennet. He's not the serious relationship type. He goes out to the clubs almost every night to find a woman to bring home. Then in the morning, he kicks them out and never sees them again. I want better for you."

"You aren't telling me anything I don't know, Damon. Bennet's been completely honest with me about his views on relationships. We're not serious anyway. We're hanging out, getting to know one another. Just like you and Jazz when you two got together. There is no

87

label for us. We're just two single people enjoying each other's company. I'm not looking for marriage or a commitment. Is that so bad?"

"Look," I hear him let out a long sigh. "I've said my piece on the matter; what you do is up to you. Jazz just wanted me to call and see if you were going to be staying here."

"I think I'm fine right where I am."

"At Bennet's?"

"That's right."

"Alright. I hope you know what you're doing."

I laugh. I never know what I'm doing. "I do," I tell him.

"Alright. Bye, Mads. Wait, one more thing…just don't bury your head in the sand about what you're doing. Things like this…they never end well, Maddie."

"Bye, Damon." I hang up the phone and drop it onto the couch.

I lay my head down, thinking things over, and end up drifting off to sleep.

I wake to a soft kiss on my shoulder blade. I groan and roll over with a smile.

"Good morning," Bennet teases, rubbing his hand up and down my thigh. "Did a day of pampering wear you out?"

I laugh and nod. "Sounds crazy, doesn't it?"

"Anything is tiring if you're not used to it. Even being pampered." He bends over and presses a kiss to my stomach, right next to my bellybutton. I didn't realize my shirt had been worked up in my sleep.

I nod. "I'm starving."

He holds out his hand, and I take it to be pulled to my feet.

He leads me to the dining room, where the table is all prepared. I take my seat and pick up the beer that he set out.

"You never told me why you fired Quinn."

He quickly glances at me but then back to his plate. "She tried to seduce me," he says in a serious tone.

I can't hold back my laughter. "What? Seriously?"

He nods, now wearing a small smirk.

"Did she touch you? Did you kiss?"

He shakes his head. "Absolutely not. She just started taking off her clothes right in front of me."

I shake my head. "I'll never understand your life."

"What? You mean that people in your life don't just strip to get you to sleep with them?"

"No," I say around my laughter.

"Does that make you jealous?"

"What? That she tried to seduce you or that you have people throwing themselves at you every day and I don't?"

He snorts. "If you only paid attention." He shakes his head.

"To what?" I ask, smile still in place.

"Do you not see the looks you get when you walk through the office?"

"What looks?"

"I bet almost all of the men in the office would fuck you if you'd let them."

I purse my lips together. "Really? Well, I may need to rethink our arrangement now that I know I have options," I tease.

He lets out a quiet chuckle. "You have more options than you realize."

I'm not sure what that means, but I let it slide, opting to eat the delicious dinner in front of me that he prepared.

"Where'd you learn to cook?" I ask around a mouthful of the best mac and cheese I've ever had in my life.

"My mom made sure I knew how. My dad was born into money, but she didn't have much of anything growing up. She had to cook and do laundry and all of it. So, when I started getting old enough to do things, she made sure that I would have the skills I needed in life."

I smile. "She sounds like a smart woman."

He nods. "She is. I have no idea what in the hell she sees in my dad, but they've been happily married for nearly forty years now."

"Maybe only she sees his soft side. I'm sure if you asked around the office, nobody would know this side of you."

He laughs.

"What?"

He shakes his head as he chews his food. "I just thought about my dad having two different lives: one for work and one for play. I never thought of it that way."

"Guess it runs in the family."

We sit and have a nice dinner where we talk and share things from our past. I tell him about some of my childhood stories growing up with Jazz and Damon, about the parties we wormed our way into, and the trouble we caused. He tells me some trouble he got into himself. We laugh and drink for most of the night, never leaving the dining room table. Talking to him is easy, much easier than it used to be. He used to intimidate me. First, by being the badass boxer he is, and then by turning out to be my boss and the person that could fire me. But now, he's not either of those things. He's just Bennet, and I love spending time with him.

"What do you say to a swim?" he asks, finishing off his beer and setting it down.

"It's a little cold outside, isn't it?"

"I have an indoor pool. And it's heated." His green eyes hold a gleam of amusement.

"I don't have a suit," I say with a shrug.

"Neither do I," he replies, standing and taking my hand.

He leads me down a long hallway in the back of the house I've never seen before. But I've only been in his house a few times, and I never snooped. At the end of the hallway, he pushes through another door, and the smell of chlorine hits my nose. I inhale it deeply.

"I've always loved that smell," I say, walking into the room behind him. One wall is solid brick, but the other side is nothing but windows, so you can see into the back yard. The rooftop is also glass. The lights are dimmed low, but the bright lights in the pool illuminate everything. Outside, the landscaping lights are on, spotlighting beautiful flowers and perfectly manicured shrubs.

I reach for the hem of my shirt and start to lift it, but he stops me.

"Oh no, the stripping is for me to do," he says, pulling my shirt up and over my head. When it hits the concrete floor, his lips find mine. I quickly get to work on tearing off his shirt and unfastening his jeans. He kicks them to the side while he pushes mine down my legs.

"Oh," I say, breaking the kiss. "I'm not supposed to get wet. It will remove my tan." I look down at my tan body. Seeing it is still quite alarming to me.

"I like your ivory skin better anyway," he says, pulling his shorts down and jumping in the pool.

I laugh, strip off my panties and jump in, headfirst. When I pop up out of the water, I can see an off-putting color swirling in the water around me.

"Told ya," I say, looking down at the water.

He laughs and jumps for me, trying to pull me under the water. I quickly swim away.

"Do you swim laps?" I ask when our roughhousing cools down.

He's floating on his back. "I used to every morning when I was training."

"Let's do it now. Let's race."

He smiles. "You're on."

We both back up to the far side of the pool.

"On your mark. Get set. Go!" I yell, and we both take off.

For the first half, we're neck and neck. He swims fast, but I stay strong. It's somewhere around the second half that I start to lose steam and fall behind.

He smacks the edge of the pool. "I win." He turns around to see me doggy paddling my way over. He lets out a deep laugh as he reaches for me and pulls me into his arms. "Out of shape?"

I'm breathless. "I haven't gone swimming for a long time. I did pretty good there at the start. I figured all the boxing would help me, but man, swimming kicks your ass!"

I hold on around his neck and wrap my legs around his waist. His hands land on my ass as he leans in and kisses me. I close my eyes, and the next thing I know, he has me pinned to the corner of the pool. His hands cup my ass, gently massaging as they move up my back and down to my thighs. Somehow, one hand ends up between us, rubbing against my clit.

I break the kiss. "I'm ready for bed," I whisper against his lips.

He brings his mouth back to mine and holds me against him as he walks us up the stairs and out of the pool. He doesn't worry about towels or the fact that we're dripping water all over his house. He carries me all the way up to his room and drops me onto his bed.

BENNET

I should care more about keeping the house clean now that I'm in between maids, but when I'm around her, I lose my mind. I can't think of anything but her and the way she makes me feel: like I'm eighteen again, falling in love for the first time, feeling everything for the first time. It's intoxicating.

I carry her up to my room, dripping water the whole way. I don't stop kissing her until I'm dropping her on my bed and crawling up her beautiful body. Now that all the tan has washed off, she has her radiant ivory glow back. Her cheeks are pink, her lips plump and red. She's absolutely breathtaking with her dark hair wet and clinging to both our bodies. My hands massage her full tits, and my hips grind against hers. She's already so wet for me, I slide my fingers between her folds with ease as her breath hitches in her throat and she grips me tighter. All it would take is one rock of my hips, and I'd be sliding deep inside her. But I'm not ready for that yet. I want to taste her.

I work myself down her body, sucking, licking, and kissing my away across her goose bump prickled skin. Her breathing picks up; a small moan tumbles from her lips. When my mouth closes in on her clit, she gasps, and her hand grips the top of my head. Her hips rock against my face, and I have to hold them down to keep her still.

Holding her down only seems to tease her more. I let her go with one hand but use it to slide two fingers inside her sheath. She says my name in a moan of approval. As my mouth and hand work her over, her moans get louder with each thrust and lick. Finally, her muscles are squeezing against my fingers while her whole body stiffens. Her nails are digging into the mattress, and my name is all she can say. I wait until I feel her loosen up, then pull away.

"Wait, no," she says, but already I'm sliding into her, and she can't argue. My hands hold firm on her hips while I rock against her, giving us both everything we need.

––––––

WE BOTH FINISH out the workweek, and I have her in my bed every night. We go to work together every day. I'm starting to understand what Phillip was saying, about always having your best friend with you. It's something I didn't even know I wanted, but it's turning out to be something I need. When Friday rolls around, we leave the office and come home to get ready for the gala—it's a boring function my father throws every year to celebrate another year of his company being on top. I've always hated going, but I have a feeling this year will be much more fun with Maddie on my arm.

She goes into the guest room to shower and dress while I do the same in my room, the room we've been sharing. I shower, shave, and dress in my tux. I walk out of the room and knock on her door.

"Just a sec," she calls out.

A few moments later, she's opening the door, looking sexy as hell. Her body is enveloped in red silk that hangs on every curve of her luscious body. Her long hair is in loose curls over her shoulder, and her pouty lips are painted a dark red. Her eyes are what get me though. A dark cat-eye wing is swept across her lid, and her mile-long lashes are fanned out in a beautiful frame of black that makes them pop. I swear, they're so blue they're almost clear. They remind me of a glacier.

"You look…" I start, but I'm unable to finish.

"Thank you." She smiles, and a slight blush creeps up her neck. "Would you zip me up?" She spins around, and her milky skin teases me. I want nothing more than to rip this dress off and stay here where I can be buried in her all night. I shake the thoughts away, knowing that if I don't go, I'll be getting a visit from my father.

I reach for the zipper on the dress, and as I pull it up, I let my fingers glide along her soft skin. It causes goosebumps to prickle her flesh. When she turns around, her cheeks are flushed, and her lips are parted.

I shoot her a grin. "Don't give me that look, or you won't leave the house looking like this." I motion toward her.

She laughs. "How will I look?"

"Your lipstick will be smeared clear across your face, your hair will be a wreck, and your dress will probably be ripped because I'm too impatient to use zippers."

She laughs and shakes her head. "Let's go before all this gets wrecked." She motions down her body.

I hold out my arm, and she takes it as I lead her down the stairs.

The new manager my assistant hired opens the door for us, and I lead her outside and into the waiting limo I reserved for tonight. The driver is standing by the door, and he opens it as we approach. She slides in first, and then I follow. I can't keep my eyes off her ass until she sits down. The driver closes the door behind us, and her perfume floats in my direction. It clouds my head and has me stretching the crotch of my pants.

I move to the floor, getting down on my knees in front of her.

"What are you doing?" she asks.

I shake my head. "I can't wait. I have to have you now. Scoot."

She giggles but scoots her butt to the edge of the seat and works her dress up her legs. When all the frill of her dress is out of my way, I see that she's completely bare underneath.

I arch an eyebrow. "Came prepared, did you?" I ask, freeing myself from my pants and pushing them down to my knees.

"I know how you are," she says, just as I'm sliding my tongue between her folds. I don't take my time enjoying her like I normally do; I'm a man possessed. I lap at her as I crook a finger inside her, warming her up for my cock. I work myself free with my other hand, already so hard I'm ready to tear through the seams of my pants.

I pull her hips toward mine as I thrust into her. Already, she's tightening up around me. We're both so wound up, I know it will only take minutes before we're both calling each other's names. Her nails dig into my back as she bites her lower lip. Soft moans and whimpers escape her mouth even though it's clear she's trying to be quiet. I rock against her a couple more times before we're both falling together. I pull out quickly and grab a tissue out of the box on the next seat over, spilling everything I have inside me.

I laugh as I dry up the mess and toss the tissue into the trash. "It's like they knew we were coming."

She laughs and shakes her head before pulling a matching red lace thong from her clutch. She pulls the panties up her long, toned legs before getting her dress back into position. "I'm wearing silk, so can't exactly stay bare," she explains with a little wink.

I take my seat next to her and put myself back in place while tucking in my shirt to look presentable. We get all fixed up just as the limo is slowing down.

"Are you ready?" I ask.

She lets out a deep breath and nods. "As I'll ever be."

I pick up her hand and press a kiss to the top. "Don't be nervous. Mom isn't bad, and I doubt my dad will say anything to either of us."

"Your parents are going to be here?" Her eyes grow wide with fear.

"Of course, it's a gala for the company. I told you that. He's the founder."

"Oh, my God. How could you not tell me that?"

I place my hands on either side of her face. "Shh, it's okay. There's nothing to worry about. I'll be with you the whole time."

She nods but still looks as nervous as can be. Her blue eyes are dashing around like crazy, and her hands are visibly shaking. "Okay," she breathes out.

The driver opens the door for us and I step out, holding out my hand to help her out as well. We walk across the red carpet, and a few pictures are snapped as we walk into the big brick building. She leans closer.

"No one from work will be here, right?" she whispers, squeezing my hand tighter.

"Nobody you work with, sweetheart. Like I said before, it's mostly for the higher-ups, investors, and my father, of course. Relax. You have nothing to worry about," I assure her.

Instead of making my presence known, I take her to the open bar, and we both order a drink. As we stand, enjoying our cocktails, I look around. There are many people I see from the board; they're all standing in a circle, talking shop while drinking their liquor. Their wives are all sitting around a circular table, gossiping and trying to find out who has the most money, I'm sure. I keep scanning over the place and find my mother and father, sitting at a table at the head of the room. There are people dancing on the ballroom floor, waiters walking about to deliver champagne and hors d'oeuvres.

My father looks up, and his blue-gray eyes land on mine. I see him motion with his head, letting Mom know I'm here. When I see him push his chair back, I lean toward Maddie.

"Brace yourself. My parents have spotted us, and they're coming over."

She quickly throws back her drink and starts smoothing her dress down.

"Bennet," my father says, walking up and holding out his hand to shake.

I nod my head and shake his hand. "Father." I step closer and give my mom a hug. "Mom."

"How have you been?" Dad asks. "Have you seen your sister? I was hoping she'd attend this year."

"I'm doing well," I reply, ignoring his question about Val because that's always a sensitive subject. "Mom, Dad, this is Maddie, a close friend of mine. She works at the company and is quickly rising in her department."

Dad looks over at her. "And what department would that be?"

"Date configuration and analysis, sir."

His brows lift with surprise. My dad is one of those old-school assholes that still thinks women belong behind a desk, answering a phone—if they insist on working, but should be at home with children. "Well, isn't that lovely."

She smiles and nods once, not sure if that's a compliment or just a basic statement.

I feel like I'm reaching for something to say. "She's been waiting for a position to open up for a year now. Finally, she got her chance to shine and proved to be an incredible asset to the company. With one report, she was put where she belongs. She's already doubled our new app sales and has nearly tripled our profit margins by helping us redesign the website."

Dad seems to be bored listening to me talk her up.

"Please, excuse me," he says, not responding to me. "Richard!" he hollers after someone walking by, and he quickly chases after him, leaving Mom standing with us.

"Why don't you two sit with me at our table," Mom says, motioning toward her table in the front of the room.

We follow her over, and I pull out both their chairs before taking a seat for myself.

"Have you talked to Valerie lately?" Mom asks, picking up her glass of wine.

I nod. "I talked to her on the phone last week. I need to call her again. I've had a job open up that I think she'd be perfect for."

Mom rolls her green eyes and pushes her red hair away from her face. "You know your sister…"

I nod. "I do, but I think she's coming around."

I look up to find Maddie swirling the liquid around inside her glass, looking as bored as can be.

"So, tell me. Are you two dating?" Mom asks, looking back and forth between me and Maddie.

I laugh out of nervousness. "No, just thought that she needs to get her face and name known. She's very good at what she does."

"That's nice," Mom says. "Whatever happened to that last girl you were seeing?"

I wave her off. "That was nothing."

"Well, what about Quinn? You know, she would make a wonderful wife. Why you fired her, I'll never know. I put her in your home for a reason, you know."

My eyes nearly bulge out of my skull. "Excuse me?"

"Well, I know how you are, Bennet. You want everything you can't have. I figured if I put someone in your home and told you to keep your hands to yourself, you'd do exactly what I told you not to. She's very beautiful, don't you think?"

"I... I..." I can't find the words I'm reaching for. I glance over at Maddie and can see her growing more uncomfortable by the minute. "No, I don't think. And since when do you want me marrying a maid?"

She laughs. "She wasn't a maid, silly boy. She's a house manager and Sandra's granddaughter. She wanted her to spend a year working before she left her with any of the family money. You know, so she would learn the value."

"This is crazy, Mother." I shake my head and pick up my drink, throwing it back. "Please, excuse us." I push my chair back and stand, holding out my hand for Maddie. She stands and slides her hand around my elbow.

"Would you please dance with me?"

She smiles sweetly even though I'm sure she's about as comfortable as a whore in church. "Of course."

I walk her to the dance floor and pull her against me. "I'm so sorry. I had no idea she'd do any of this."

"It's fine, Bennet."

"I knew my mother was hassling me to settle down, but I honestly never thought she'd plant someone in my house like that. I mean, who does that?"

She shrugs. "Maybe you should just tell her that we're dating. You know, to get her off your back."

I shake my head. "No, that would only start the 'when will you get married and have children' talk again. No, it's better this way. Trust me."

She lets the subject drop as we dance around the floor. I enjoy holding her close, but it annoys me that I can't lean over and kiss her or touch her in any way that may signal that we're more than what we're pretending to be.

We dance through three different songs played by the orchestra before we break for a drink. While we're standing at the bar, a board member bumps into me.

"Oh, excuse me, Bennet," Tom says.

"Don't worry about it. How's the wife and kids?" I ask, just to be polite.

He nods. "The wife is on vacation in the Keys. My son just graduated from Harvard, and my daughter just started at Yale. Everything is good." He looks over at Maddie. "Who's this beautiful young lady?"

"This is Madeline Strickland. She's in the company's data configuration department."

"Oh, very nice. Are you dipping into the company ink?" he asks with a smirk.

I laugh nervously at his rather crude and outdated pun. "No, not at all. Madeline is here with me to get to know the company and everyone involved a little bit better. We're just coworkers."

He pats me on the shoulder. "I'm just teasing you. Now, I must get back over to my date for the evening." He motions to a young blonde, that's not his wife, sitting across the room.

"Enjoy your evening," I tell him, turning back to Maddie. She's holding her drink between two hands and staring off into space.

I lean closer. "Are you getting bored?"

Her eyes blink, and she forces a smile onto her face. "I'm fine. But I'm not feeling very well. Please, excuse me." She places her glass on the bar and heads for the restroom.

I stand and watch her go, questioning if the events of the evening are getting to her or if she's really not feeling well. I want to chase after her, take her home if need be, but again, I'm afraid someone will notice us acting differently and start to put things together. Instead, I hang back, drinking my cocktail and waiting for her to return.

13

MADDIE

Walking to the bathroom, I feel the tears burning my eyes. But I refuse to let them fall. I don't know what's wrong with me. I'm getting exactly what I wanted, but along the way, something changed.

Bennet has been introducing me as a friend, a coworker, an employee: all things that I am. But the things I want to be, and the thing I'm not is his girlfriend. I can't be mad at him. He's only doing what he agreed to. I mean, I'm the one that asked to keep things simple before we got together, but now, I want more, and I hate myself for it.

I'm not a relationship kind of girl. I like having my own life. I like when the guy I'm seeing enjoys having his own life. I like being able to meet up in the middle and enjoy spending time together with no strings attached. So why have I suddenly changed? And how can I make it go away? When I walk out of this bathroom, I have to have my fake face back in place. I can't tell Bennet any of this. I know how he feels, and I refuse to give him an ultimatum.

And even if everything came to light, what would I do about work? I'm not the kind of girl who sleeps with the boss. When and if I do get into a committed relationship, I don't want to have to hide my life from my friends at work. And I don't want everyone else spreading rumors about how I got the job I did. God, everything is such a mess.

I dry my eyes and slip out of the bathroom. As I walk toward the doors, I see Bennet still at the bar, but a woman with big boobs and blonde hair is keeping his attention, so he doesn't see me. I exit the building and turn left down the sidewalk, just needing some time and space, not to mention air to clear my head. There's a bench on the sidewalk, and I sit down, pulling my phone from my clutch.

"Hello?" Jazz answers.

"I'm so stupid, Jazz. I don't know what to do."

"What? Why? What's wrong?"

I take a clearing breath. "I'm falling in love with him," I confess.

"That's great, Mads, but why do you sound upset?"

"Bennet and I agreed to keep things casual, to not do the whole relationship thing. I can't tell him how I feel, but I know letting this go on will only make it that much harder in the end. I don't know what to do."

"Oh, honey. I think we both know there's only one thing you can do."

"Date other men and hope it wears off?" I ask, only half-joking.

She laughs. "No. Tell him how you feel. If your feelings have changed, maybe his have too."

I feel my shoulders fall with the deep breath that leaves my lips. "You think so?"

"I know so."

"Here you are. Why didn't you tell me you were coming outside?" Bennet asks, walking up to me.

I hang up the phone without a word and slip it back into my clutch. "I just needed some air. It's too stuffy in there."

He nods as he sits next to me. "I know it is."

"I didn't want to interrupt. I saw you talking with that woman."

He waves me off. "That was nothing. My mother sent her over. Another match-making attempt, I'm sure."

I laugh. "At least she knows your type."

I see him look at me from the corner of my eye. "She's not my type."

My brow lifts. "Big boobs, leggy, blonde hair: that isn't your type?"

"Nope. I prefer dark hair and ivory skin. Thick red lips, soft skin, and icy blue eyes."

Slowly, I look over at him. Our eyes lock, and for the first time, I think I see something brewing behind them: love.

Does Bennet love me? Would us getting together be such a bad thing? I mean, it's not really any different than what we're already doing. Everything I do with him outside of work is hidden from the people I work with.

"Bennet?"

"Hmm?"

"Something has changed."

He nods. "I know."

"You do?" I ask, not sure if he understands what I'm talking about.

"I do. Something has changed with us this week. I've never spent this much time with a woman before. I feel like the more time we spend together, the more I want you with me. And that scares me."

"What do you think we should do?"

"I've been asking myself that question."

I turn my head and look at the building directly in front of me, not happy that we still don't have an answer for our problem, but at the same time happy that I've gotten it off my chest.

He holds out his hand. "Come on. Let's get out of here."

"You can do that?"

"I can do whatever I want."

I place my hand in his, and he pulls me to his side. He leads me back to the front of the building and into our waiting limo. All the while, our pictures are being snapped by cameramen behind the ropes.

We both slide into the seat, and the moment the door is closed, the driver hits the gas. The cab of the car is dark, all but the running lights along the top. It's not bright enough to do anything like read, but it's enough light that I can see his face.

"Did it bother you when I told people that we are just friends or coworkers?" he asks, voice low and unsure.

I nod. "It did, and I hated that it did. First off, it's only been a couple weeks since we met. I shouldn't feel this way. Secondly, we both agreed to keep things casual. And lastly, we'd never work out. I mean, we're already hiding what we're doing from everyone in our lives. We can't do that forever."

He just sits and listens to my concerns, nodding his head as I tick off the reasons we won't work long-term.

"So, what do you suggest?" he asks.

I shrug. "I was hoping you'd have the answer to that."

"The way I see it, we have three options. We keep doing what we're doing, we break up and go our separate ways, or we get serious and say to hell with the consequences."

I laugh and roll my eyes. "If it were only that easy. You have these feelings too, right?"

He nods. "It's all new to me, but I know the way I feel with you, I've never felt with anyone else."

"So, you don't want to go our separate ways?"

"No, I don't want that. Do you want that?" he asks, suddenly looking up at me.

"No," I breathe out, shaking my head. "But can you keep doing what we're doing without knowing that it's going to last? I mean, that's what this is. It's a relationship with no promises. What if I spend the next fifty years with you and one day decide that I'm done?"

"Marriage doesn't mean that won't happen either, Maddie," he says, picking up my hand and holding it.

I nod. "To me, it does. I never wanted to get married because to me, it means forever. And I never found a man I thought I could be with forever… until you."

He turns his head so that he's looking at the rain that's just starting to speckle the window.

"Are you saying that if I don't want marriage, that we're over?" he asks.

"No," I reply, causing him to turn and look at me. "I'm saying that if it's off the table completely, if there's absolutely no chance of ever being your forever, then it's over. But if there's even a small part of you that thinks you could spend the rest of your life with me, I'd love to stay by your side and wait with you—wait for us both to be ready for that step."

His eyes start bouncing around the inside of the cab, looking at anything and everything while he thinks it over. Finally, he looks back at me, our eyes meeting in the darkened limo. His hand slowly releases mine and moves up to cup my cheek. "I never thought I'd want any of this. I can't promise that I won't fuck up from time to time, but I do promise to be here, by your side, and let things between us grow. I won't fight it. I won't hold back. I'll give you everything I have to give in the moment, and if things between us start moving in that direction, we'll follow that road. Sound like a deal?"

"So, we're together, like a couple?"

He smiles. "If that's what you want."

"What about family and work?"

"We'll tell our families; work won't change," he promises.

Happiness fills my chest, and I smile wide, jumping into his lap and pressing my mouth to his. His hands land on my hips, pushing me down against his groin, where I rock myself back and forth across it. I bite his lower lip as I pull away.

"Mr. Windsor, are you happy to see me?"

He grins. "I'm happy to be able to say that you're all mine." He starts moving back in.

"I've been yours since you walked into that ring," I whisper, kissing him with as much passion and love that can pour out of me.

We only pull apart long enough to get from the limo to the house, but the second we're inside, he's spinning me around and pushing me against the door. His lips are against mine, and his hands are moving up and down my back, trying to get it unzipped. Suddenly, I feel a jerk and hear the fabric ripping.

I gasp as I break our kiss. My eyes meet his, and he grins. "I told you I'm too impatient for zippers." He pulls again, and the dress splits at the seams. The second he drops it and it falls around my feet, he picks me up against him, moving his lips back to mine. I wrap my legs around his hips and my arms around his neck as he carries me up the stairs and into his room.

———

WHEN I OPEN my eyes Saturday morning, I find Bennet laying next to me, still naked from the night before and eyes shining with happiness.

"Have you been watching me?" I ask with a sleepy smile.

He nods. "I couldn't help myself," he whispers, leaning in for a kiss.

I kiss him quickly but pull away, not wanting to chase him off with my morning breath. "What's the plans for today?" I ask, stretching.

"I thought we'd hit up the races tonight. What do you think?"

I smile wide. "I'd love to. Are you going to race?"

"Not tonight. I thought that maybe we could invite Jazz and Damon to go with us. You know, since we discussed telling our family."

"Really?"

He nods. "I told you, I want this. I've done this thing with many women, but I never had the urge to stay in bed all day with them like I do with you." He cups my cheek. "Something's different about you. I can't shake it, and I don't want to." He leans in slowly, pressing his lips to mine.

———

WE'RE PULLING into the races just as the sun is beginning to set. We park, hit up the concession stand, and then have a seat on the bleachers. I'm just finishing up with my hot pretzel when Jazz and Damon walk up.

"Hey," I greet them, standing and pulling Jazz in for a hug. "Thanks for coming."

She smiles. "We would've been here sooner, but Damon needed some persuading."

I shake my head and roll my eyes. "Still not happy about this hook-up, huh?"

She shrugs one shoulder. "He's coming around."

Bennet stands up to greet them. "Damon," he says, holding out his hand to shake.

Damon nods but doesn't reply. He does shake his hand, though.

We all sit down and watch as the cars speed down the track, but nobody talks. Finally, I turn to Jazz. "I'm going to go grab some drinks. Want to help me?"

She nods. "Sure."

When we get to the bottom of the bleachers, she leans in. "So, how'd it go last night? Did you tell him how you felt?"

I nod. "I did, and to my surprise, he feels the same way. We're official, and this is us breaking the news to you guys."

She laughs aloud. "That's great, Mads."

"But Damon…" I let my sentence break off.

She bumps my shoulder with hers. "He'll come around. He's just worried that Bennet will use you and leave you heartbroken."

I let out a deep breath. "Why? Because it's Bennet?"

She nods. "He said that Bennet has never committed to anything in his life, that he bounces from one girl to the next, that as soon as he gets tired of them, he's pulling away. I think the only thing that will change his mind is time, you know? Once he sees that you and Bennet are serious and have been together for a while, things will be fine."

I laugh. "Great, so I only have to live through ten years of his attitude."

She moves her head from side to side, thinking it over. "Maybe only five?" Her face wrinkles like even she's not sure.

We both laugh, and I bump my shoulder into hers. "I don't know how I get myself into these messes, but they always find me."

"You're not the only one," she agrees.

"Have you picked any baby names yet?" I ask as we wait in line.

"We discussed a few but haven't settled on any. We don't have to have our hearts set on any until we find out the sex of the baby."

"How have you been feeling? Have you had morning sickness really bad?"

"Every morning. It's killing me. But I figured out that I could drink some ginger ale and eat a Snickers, and I'd be fine within the hour."

I laugh. "This baby must have a sweet tooth."

She nods. "I was never big on a lot of sweets until I got pregnant. And I almost always had a salad for lunch, but suddenly, I can't stand it. I'll open the box, and the smell will hit me. I've puked every time."

"This baby has to have some of my genes. You just described me to a T," I joke.

"Well, you are the aunt."

I lean my head against her shoulder. "I know I haven't said this much, but I'm happy for you and Damon. I am."

She offers a small smile. "I know but thank you for saying it."

14

BENNET

When the girls leave to grab some drinks, I figure this is my chance to talk to Damon. I scoot toward him. "Listen, man," I start, but he turns toward me, cutting me off.

"All the women in the city and you go after my sister? My baby sister?" He has a tick in his jaw that tells me he's furious.

"I didn't know she was your sister," I admit.

"Yeah, right. Something tells me you knew exactly what you were doing."

"Really? Is that how you think of me? I do nothing but go around doing things that would hurt the people I care about?" I pause to let him respond, but he doesn't.

"The second my eyes landed on hers, something called to me. Something about her made my heart race; it made my stomach tighten. Just looking at her, I knew she was the one I wanted."

"That's my point. The one you *wanted*. You can't tell me that this didn't start because of your dick. All you wanted was a good time."

"So what if I did? Are you saying that you weren't attracted to Jazz?"

"What? No!"

"That's my point. Every relationship, every marriage, it all started because two people were attracted to each other. And just like any other couple out there, once we started spending time together, things have grown past the sexual stage. I enjoy her company. Just seeing her smile makes me smile. I want to spend the rest of my life with her, man."

We both go silent for a moment, letting everything sink in and also taking a moment to cool off.

"Are you saying that you two are in a relationship? Like an actual committed relationship?"

"Yes, that's why we invited you here. We made the decision last night and wanted to start letting our friends and family know."

"You're not out banging other people?"

"I haven't even looked at another woman since I met Maddie," I admit.

"And how's this going to work with the office and your family? Because I know your father and Maddie isn't the type of woman he wants you with."

I wave my hand in the air. "Screw my dad."

His head jerks in my direction. "What if he tells you to dump her or to give up the company? Are you willing to do that?"

"Absolutely," I say without hesitation. "We both know how little that company means to me. I have enough money to live comfortably for the rest of my life, the rest of our lives."

He nods. "Okay. I'll stop fighting this then. But I swear to God, Bennet, if you hurt her, I will kill you. Understand?" He holds up his hand to shake.

I slap mine into his. "I wouldn't expect anything less," I agree.

"So, why aren't you out there racing tonight?" He motions toward the track.

"I haven't raced in a while. I ran the other day, and my time sucked. Plus, I'd rather sit in the stands with Maddie and watch her experience it all for the first time. It's like a whole new world to her."

He laughs. "Yeah, this is one place she never tried following me to —the only place I could get a break."

"Tagalong, was she?"

His eyes grow wide. "You have no idea. And Jazz was always right alongside her. I couldn't go anywhere without the two of them."

I smile and turn my attention back to the track, wishing I'd met Damon sooner. I know that if I would've met Maddie before college, things would've been different for me. I never would have gotten in so much trouble; I'd never have gotten the reputation I have now for being a player. I know I would've set eyes on her and been done.

When the girls come back, they take their seats between us, and we all watch the race. Something feels different, like the air is thinner around us. I feel like the weight of the world has been lifted from my shoulders, but then I remember we still have to tackle the hardest part: my parents.

———

"ARE YOU SURE ABOUT THIS?" Maddie asks Sunday morning as we're getting dressed for brunch.

"Everything will be fine," I say, tightening my tie.

"They've already met me, and they hate me." Her brows are arched high, and she has a little worry line between her eyes.

"They don't hate you," I insist.

"Your dad couldn't have looked less interested when you were telling him about me. And your mom, she kept trying to hook you up with other women even though she knew you were there with me. That doesn't scream *love* to me."

I place my hands on her biceps, forcing her to look at me. "It doesn't matter what they say. Nothing is going to change. Besides, no matter who I bring home to them, it will never be good enough."

She nods her head, agreeing with what I'm saying, but she doesn't look sure. She looks afraid. I kiss her quickly on the forehead and get back to dressing.

A little while later, we're pulling up to the country club. I hand over the keys to the valet and lead her inside. We're greeted by the hostess the moment we step through the door. I give her the name the reservation is under and then follow her back to the table my parents are sitting at. Dad is dressed to impress in his designer suit and blood-red power tie. My mother is dressed in her usual cream-colored dress suit. Her red hair is soft and flowing, her makeup done to perfection. They look like what you'd imagine any rich older couple to look like.

When we approach, Dad stands and shakes my hand. I lean down and press a kiss to Mom's cheek. "Mom, Dad, I know I've already introduced you, but this is my girlfriend, Madeline. Madeline, my parents, Tom and Marlyn Windsor."

Maddie smiles and shakes their hands. My parents get a nervous look on their faces but try holding back to be polite.

Once we're all seated and have drinks, Dad speaks up. "This is the same woman that was with you at the gala, correct?" he asks, pointing at her rudely.

I nod. "She is."

"Didn't you introduce her as an employee?" His features begin to twist, causing his wrinkles to appear deeper.

I clear my throat and nod. "Yes, I did. We didn't exactly have a label then. We've talked about it and decided to take the jump." I pick up her hand and squeeze it gently.

"Bennet," Mom says, "I'm worried that Madeline, here, while very beautiful, and talented from what I've heard, doesn't know the expectations of our lifestyle."

My mouth drops open.

"She hasn't been raised with money, Bennet," she points out.

"Neither were you, Mom," I argue.

"Screw that," Dad says. "I'm more worried about my company. I worked too hard for too many years to let something like this tarnish its reputation."

I hold my hand in the air, palm facing him. "Dad, I assure you, the company is fine."

"It is now, but what will happen when this comes out? I'll be accused of running a brothel." He picks up his cloth napkin from his lap and tosses it onto the table.

"Dad, that's ridiculous," I laugh out.

He stands so fast his chair topples. "Bennet, this is the most irresponsible thing you've ever done. I'm used to you putting yourself in jeopardy, but I was under the impression you were cleaning your life up. You can make bad decisions for yourself, but not for my company." He shakes his head. "Marlyn, we're leaving. Get your purse," he says, walking away.

Mom jumps up quickly, grabbing her jacket off the back of her chair and her purse. She looks me up and down, then quickly follows after my father. I look over at Maddie, expecting to see her looking upset over my family's disapproval. To my surprise, she's wearing a small grin while spreading jam on her biscuit.

"Are you smirking?" I ask, amusement filling my voice.

She shrugs. "I'm sorry. I know this isn't good, but I'm just happy that my family is the understanding of the two."

I laugh loudly, causing the people around us to give me a dirty look.

"Well, we're here. We might as well enjoy a nice brunch on my father." I lean forward and grab a biscuit for myself.

After brunch, we decide to take a walk and end up finding ourselves sitting on the beach. The sun is bright and shining, but the wind doesn't stop, so we have a nice, cool breeze. Maddie lays back and covers her eyes with her arm. The beach is crowded with everyone playing in the sand soaking in some sun, or just hanging out. Kids are flying kites, and tourists are busy walking about and taking it all in. I lay back and press a kiss to her inner bicep. She lifts her arm slightly and flashes me a smile.

"It really doesn't bother you? Your parents not loving me?"

I scoff. "I couldn't care less. All they care about is money. Who has it, who doesn't, and making damn sure everyone knows that they have more than enough of it."

"I thought you said your mom was poor?"

I nod. "She was, but she's had too many years of living large. She's forgotten where she came from."

"Do you think your dad is going to stir trouble at the office?"

My eyes cut to hers. "Would it be bad if I said I hoped so?"

She raises her brows in surprise and sits up. "You do?"

I sit up beside her and look out over the water. "I hate my job. I hate that company. It's not what I want to do with my life. I only took my position as a way to provide for myself and to get my dad off my back."

"What do you really want to do?"

I shrug. "I don't know. But not this. I don't want to sit in my office on the top floor and push papers around. I want to do something. When I leave work, I want to feel like I've done something. When I leave now, I feel I've wasted another day of my life."

"If you could live any way you wanted, where do you see us in the future?"

I allow my mind to drift, to dream—something I never do. "I see us living in the suburbs, in a nice but reasonable house. I can see myself getting up early every morning and starting the coffee while I shower. When I'm done, I sneak back into bed with you and wake you up with soft kisses."

She giggles.

"I see a couple of kids at the breakfast table while we're both rushing around to get out the door. You'll have some kind of home business—or maybe managing my newest company."

"I like the sound of that," she admits. "But the question is, what kind of company?"

I laugh. "I have no idea."

"Okay," she says, turning her body to face me. "Let's start with hobbies. You like to race, and you like to box. Which of the two could you see yourself doing?"

I move my head from one side to the other, thinking it over. "I love boxing, it's something I've never stopped doing, but it's also something that takes a toll on your body. People retire from boxing pretty young. But racing, that's something I've been thinking about getting more involved in for a long time."

Her eyes stretch wide. "Good, that's a start. You could open a garage, build drag cars."

That's not a bad idea. I've always worked on my own cars in the past, and up until here recently when I stopped racing, they've always had great times at the track.

"What could we call it?" she asks, eyes moving up to the sky as she thinks. "BW Racing?"

I laugh and shake my head. "Sure, why not? This is all just pretend, right?"

She looks at me, and her blue eyes glaze over. "Only if you want it to be."

"You think I could do it?"

She crawls into my lap and wraps her arms around my neck. "I think you can do anything, Bennet. You just have to believe it."

———

MONDAY MORNING COMES, and we both head into the office. But something feels different today. The air around me feels cold and brittle. Like one wrong word could shatter my entire existence. I can't figure out why, though. Maddie and I are in a great place. She finally received her insurance check in the mail this morning and now has money to find herself a new apartment, even though I begged her not to. She agreed to put the money aside and hold onto it for a rainy day.

I haven't heard from my parents, and even though I feel like I should worry about what Dad's planning on doing, I'm not worried in the slightest. In the past, when my dad threatened to take the company away from me, I worried because I had no idea what else I could do. But after that talk with Maddie, she made me realize that I have unlimited possibilities. I could go into boxing full time. I could move into racing, travel the world racing cars, and making money. I could open a garage, like she suggested, and build and sell drag cars. I could also just take some time off, live in a respectable house, and enjoy the time I have with her. I could look into starting something new, dabbling in everything as an investor. I have the money to do anything I want.

I guess that's one thing Dad gave me. I've made more money in the time I've been CEO than most people make in ten years. And I didn't just spend that money either. I've saved it, letting it gain interest. I've invested it, and my investments usually bring in a normal person's yearly salary in a month's time. I don't have to work for the rest of my life if I don't want to. I could just sit back and collect money. Realizing this is liberating.

I'm no longer held back by my father and his wishes, or threats. For the first time in my life, I can do whatever I want. I walk into the office with a smile on my face.

"Good morning, Sarah," I say as I approach my office doors.

She stands. "Mr. Windsor, your father is in your office."

A long breath leaves my lips. "Thank you, Sarah. Would you mind bringing in some coffee, please?"

"Of course." She runs toward the break room to fulfill my wish.

I push through the doors and find my father standing in my office, back facing the door as he gazes out over the city. He spins around when he hears me come in.

"I used to look out this window every day for thirty years; did you know that?"

I nod as I come to a stop next to him. "I did."

"I was here at eight o'clock on the dot, and I didn't leave until nearly seven each night. And look at you, wandering in at nine."

A rush of air leaves me. "What's this about, Dad? Is this really about Madeline and me, or are you just looking for any excuse to come back to work?"

The door opens, and Sarah walks in with two cups of coffee. I walk over to my desk and sit down, taking a sip. When Sarah leaves the room, Dad sits across from me.

"You don't have the drive to run this company. You don't have the will nor the want. You're just pacifying me."

I nod. "I've recently come to realize that myself."

His brows perk up, and his eyes grow wide. "You're finally admitting it?" He lets out a bitter sounding laugh.

"Dad, this was your company. You started this business from the house, and when it grew to be bigger than you imagined it would ever be, you moved into this building. You've seen it through all the way. In a way, it's more your child than I am," I tell him. "I don't think anyone will ever run it the way you did, but that doesn't mean that it's not taken care of."

His eyes meet mine, but he doesn't respond.

"If you want to come back, I won't fight you. If you want me to step down, I will. Out of respect for you. I respect your decisions to do whatever you want in life, but it'd be nice if you afforded me the same luxury."

"Are you talking about that girl? What's her name?" he starts reaching, trying to remember.

"Madeline," I remind him. "And yes, you can't use my relationship with Madeline as a reason to kick me out of the business. I'm doing a good job here. It's not a job I love, but it is one I don't want to see fail... because it's yours. I won't let you down like that."

"My only problem with this woman is that she's your employee, Bennet. I don't care if she grew up in a penthouse or a high rise. The fact of the matter is you're letting yourself tarnish my business. When word gets out that the CEO of Windsor Wealth Management found his wife working in the godforsaken mailroom..." He rolls his eyes at the thought.

"How'd you know she was in the mailroom?" I ask, perplexed since I never mentioned it for this reason.

"After you brought her to the gala, I did a little digging. She was in the mailroom, and once you laid eyes on her, you gave her a better job. That's not how we handle our promotions in this company. Decisions aren't decided by the flavor of the week, Bennet." He stands, towering over me since I'm still sitting down.

Just hearing him use the term *flavor of the week* makes me want to laugh. I didn't even know he knew the term, but the fact that he's leaning over me with his face growing red puts an end to the amusement I've found.

He points his finger in my direction, wagging it like I'm a child that's being scolded. "You have a choice to make: dump the girl and rid this company of her—fire her, pay her off, whatever you have to do—or you can keep the girl and resign. The decision is yours. You have one week." He spins around to leave. "One week, Bennet. If you haven't made your decision by then, I will make the decision for you." He walks out, slamming the door behind him.

15

MADDIE

I'm sitting at my desk, looking over some numbers when Brian walks in. "Look what's being passed around the office," he says, dropping the company newsletter on my desk.

I pick it up, looking over the cover and realizing the image on the front is of Bennet's mother and father the night of the gala. "This gets handed out every month. What about it?"

"Turn to page eight," he says with a smirk as he leans against my desk.

I flip to page eight, and front and center is a picture of Bennet and me, from last Friday night at the gala.

"Looks like someone is screwing the boss," he laughs, looking smug as he leans onto my desk.

I roll my eyes and snort. "I am not. This is ridiculous." I close the small booklet and toss it back onto my desk.

He stands up and crosses his arms over his chest. "Then what were you doing with him? The rest of us weren't invited to this work function. Is that how you got this job? From the mailroom to data configuration; that's a pretty big jump, don't you think?"

I close my eyes and take a deep breath. "I've been in line for this position for a year, ever since you put in for a transfer before you decided against it. They hired me to fill your position, then stuck me in the mailroom when you changed your mind," I tell him, feeling anger burning its way up my chest.

"Yet, you got this job even though I'm not going anywhere. I think Mr. Windsor was impressed by you, not your work." He lets out a deep laugh before leaving the office we share.

I throw myself back into my seat and rub my temples with my fingertips, hoping to massage the anger away. I can't believe this. This is exactly what I didn't want to happen. There's no proof that we're sleeping together, but they do know that I'm at least friendly with him. That could be reason enough to get a promotion. It doesn't matter what I say. They won't believe me. They'll choose to believe the lie going around because it's more interesting.

I pick up the booklet and step out of the office. The second I do, everyone is looking at me. They're standing in groups, all of them with the newsletter in hand. Some are whispering back and forth, and others are just downright staring at me.

I push myself to keep walking. As I round the corner, I bump into someone. I stumble backward and look up to see Jen, the office gossip.

"Oh, hey, Maddie. I saw your picture with Mr. Windsor." She leans in and whispers, "Is that how you got this job? Are you sleeping with him?" She laughs in my face before I push past her, heading straight for the elevator that leads to his office.

"Ms. Strickland, you can't go in there," Sarah says, trying to stop me, but I walk in his door and find him at his desk, looking at the computer.

"I'm sorry, Mr. Windsor, but she wouldn't listen," Sarah says, chasing me in.

He stands up and moves toward us. "Don't worry about it, Sarah." He turns to face me as she steps out. "What's wrong?"

I pull the newsletter out from under my arm and flip to the page. "This! This is what's wrong!" I yell, shoving the booklet his way.

He takes it from my hands and looks down at the picture. "Fuck," he mumbles, starting to pace back and forth.

"My words exactly," I agree, falling onto the couch.

"My father is going to freak the fuck out," he says, looking at me.

I snort. "Who cares about your father? This is my life we're talking about. Already they're starting in on me, saying that I slept with you to get a promotion. This is exactly what I didn't want to happen. If they don't let up, there's no way I'm going to be able to continue to work here, Bennet. This is like freshmen year all over again."

He stops and looks at me. "Who'd you sleep with freshmen year?"

I groan. "Nobody, but I'm getting bullied and picked on by all the seniors down there!" I throw my arm in the direction of his door.

"Alright. Alright. Just calm down. This is just the hot topic of the day. Just, go back home and relax. I'm sure they will all have forgotten about it by tomorrow."

I laugh. "Nobody is forgetting this, Bennet. I might as well send in my resignation now." I stand and start moving toward the door.

His hand catches mine. "Please, don't do anything rash. Just wait this out with me. We'll figure something out. Okay?"

I nod, and he leans in, pressing his lips gently against mine.

———

WHEN I GET BACK to Bennet's place, I fill the bathtub with hot, bubbly water. I light a dozen candles and scatter them around the room and dim the lights. Then, last minute, I decide a bottle of fancy wine is in order.

I wrap my robe around myself and head to the kitchen. Even though I'm not a big wine fan, I've always heard that wine drunk and beer drunk are completely different. I need a different kind of drunk right now.

I grab a bottle and quickly open it before heading back up to my bath. As I sink into the hot water, I take a sip of the cold wine. I'm pretty sure I should have let the wine breathe—or so I've heard—but I don't have time to breathe right now. Right now, I need to figure out what the fuck I'm going to do! My life is ruined. I'm going to have to find a new job. And I don't even know what this will mean for Bennet. I know students and teachers can't have a thing, but is it wrong to carry on with an employee—other than the typical taboo that's implied?

Will he lose his job? Will his dad retaliate in some way? I love Bennet, and I don't want to cost him a thing. My thinking stops right there. I love Bennet. I love Bennet!

Oh my God, what does this mean? I knew I was having stronger feelings for him, but love? That one snuck up on me.

I grab my phone and call Jazz, knowing she isn't at work today because she had a doctor's appointment.

"Hello?" she answers.

"Come over NOW!" I insist.

"What? Where?"

"Bennet's."

"Are you okay, Mads?"

I rattle off the address and tell her it's an emergency. She hangs up, promising she'll be by soon.

I'm half drunk and half pruned, still in the bath, when she walks in.

"You could've helped me out with that guard out there," she says, walking into the bathroom.

"Sorry, I'm drunk. I forgot."

"What's this about, Maddie?" she asks, concern painting her features.

I point to the counter, and she picks up the newsletter. It doesn't take her long to get to page eight. She inhales sharply.

"Oh, no," she mumbles.

"Yep."

"What? How? When?" is all she can say.

"Last Friday. There was a gala for the company. He told me I didn't have to worry because it was only for the higher-ups, that nobody that I work with would find out."

"Damn, girl. What are you going to do? Was work bad?"

I lift an eyebrow and give her a *duh* face. "Yes, it was bad. Why else would I be taking a bath and drinking wine straight from the bottle in the middle of the day?"

"What are you going to do?"

I shrug while my lip sticks out in a pout. "I have to find a new job. What else can I do?"

"I don't know, Mads. But there has to be something. I mean, you just got your dream job." She sits on the toilet seat.

I nod. "I know."

She shakes her head. "I knew you never should've gotten involved with this guy."

"What?" I jerk my head in her direction. "You've been rooting for us to make it official."

"I was just rooting for you to be happy. But this," she motions toward the newsletter.

"It's not his fault, Jazz."

She snorts. "Yeah, right. I mean, he's the CEO of the company! He should know not to dip into the company ink." She's up and pacing back and forth across the bathroom floor now.

"What's this company ink thing? Why have I never heard it before?"

"It's just a saying. You haven't heard it?" she asks, still pacing.

"Jazz, you're acting like all of this was him. I knew who he was, and I still went along with it."

"Yeah, cuz' he didn't use all his money and power against you."

"Jazmine, seriously. Stop. This isn't his fault."

"Whose side are you on, Mads?" she asks, holding her hands out at her sides.

"Whose side are you on?" I ask, sitting up in the tub.

"Yours!" she answers, motioning toward me.

"The stuff you're saying isn't my side. You're speaking Damon's side."

Her pacing stops and she freezes, forehead wrinkling as she thinks. "Oh, my God. You're right." She sits on the toilet lid. "How did this happen? I just hate that this is happening. I hate that you don't feel comfortable at work. I hate that you finally got what you've been working all this time for, and now it's being taken away. This sucks, Mads," she breaths out.

I suck in a deep breath. "I know. Maybe Bennet is right, and this will all blow over tomorrow."

She nods with a sad smile in place. "And if not, you got thick skin. You can stick it out until it does. Eventually, they'll find something new to talk about."

"You're right! I mean, it's not like I'm the first woman on the earth to fuck her boss!"

"Yeah!" she cheers me on. "Who cares? Them bitches are just jealous that they didn't think of it."

We both stop and laugh.

"I know why I'm laughing—I'm drunk. But why are you laughing?"

Her laughs turn into tears, and she rips some toilet paper off to dry her eyes as she shrugs. "I don't know. My emotions are all screwed up. I mean, I laughed when a guy in a movie died last night, and I cried when a baby said its first words on a video today. I don't know what's wrong with me."

I'm laughing as I stand and wrap my robe around my body. I move over to her and give her a hug. "Nothing is wrong with you, honey. You're just pregnant."

We both laugh again, and somehow, everything feels better. The stress of the day is gone. Anger, gone. Now, it's just me and my best friend talking and having fun like we always used to.

Jazz and I hang out for the rest of the day. She shows me updated pictures of my old house they're getting ready to move into, and we talk baby names, and how different it's going to be with her and Damon moving out of the city. They won't be far, but still, it's more than a quick cab ride away.

Jazz hasn't been gone for more than a few minutes when Bennet walks in. I'm sitting on the couch in the living room, and usually, he comes directly to me for a kiss, but today, he doesn't pay me any attention as he passes me by on his way to the study.

I frown, wondering what's going on. I stand and follow him to find him standing over the bar cart, pouring a stiff drink.

"Hey," I say, leaning against the door.

"Hey," he says, glancing over his shoulder at me.

"Hard day?" I ask, walking further into the room.

He nods. "My father came to see me today." He tips up the glass and finishes it off before pouring another.

"And?" I ask, sitting down on the leather couch.

He turns and looks over at me. "He said if I want to keep my job, I have to fire you."

"Oh," I mumble. I hate myself for causing all this mess. "I was planning on quitting anyway," I say with a shrug.

"I'm not doing it, Maddie."

I look up and see him shaking his head.

"What?"

"I'm not doing it. I won't fire you. This whole thing is crazy. I'm a grown man. He can't tell me who I can and can't date."

"Bennet," I whisper, shaking my head. I stand and close the distance between us. "I won't let you do this. I quit. That's it. You don't have to fire me. Now, you can be rid of me at the office like your dad wants, and you can keep your job. That's what he's holding over your head, right? Your job?"

He nods. "I don't want that job anyway. I want you."

I back away, shaking my head, unable to stop. "No, Bennet. I won't let you do this. I won't let you give up your career. All of this started because of me. I'm going to end it." I turn to run from the room, but he grabs me and pulls me back, his lips finding mine.

I don't break our kiss. I can't. I want him too much. I need him too much.

I wrap my arms around his neck and pull myself closer, deepening the kiss. Somewhere inside of me knows that this is our last night, even though I refuse to think about it at this moment. I don't want him to treat me as if this is the last time, but for me, it is. I've already ruined my life. I won't ruin his too.

I hear him set his glass onto the bar cart, and then his hands are on my ass, lifting me against him. My legs wrap around his waist as he carries me across the room and sets me onto the desktop. Our hands are traveling at the speed of light, ripping and pulling one another's clothes away. When we're both completely bare, he slides into me, claiming me as his forever.

Even though I never want to part from him, I know I have to. For his sake. I won't let him lose everything because of me.

He pumps into me over and over, making me call out his name and shudder with my release. I feel his cock throbbing inside of me, and he lets out a low growl just as his hips buck uncontrollably.

When his release ends, he doesn't pull out or leave me. Instead, he kisses me softly and carries me to bed. The room is dark, and I'm wrapped up in him. His fingertips are gently moving up and down my back, and I find myself reveling in his every touch, every breath, every word. Just as I'm drifting off to sleep, I hear him whisper.

"I love you, Maddie."

It causes the corners of my mouth to turn up slightly. But then I remember that I have to leave him, and my heart begins to break.

16

BENNET

I watch her sleep for as long as I can. I tell her how much she means to me, how much I adore her, how much I love her. I've never in my life said those words to another person, but when it comes to her, I know that they're true. She makes me feel freer than I've ever felt. I don't need my job, money, or this mansion. All I need is her. If she's by my side, I know we'll get through anything.

While she sleeps, I run my fingers up and down the soft skin of her arm. I brush her hair from her beautiful face. She's captivating. The way her eyelashes fan out across her cheeks, the way her lips pooch out in a pout, the soft whimpers and deep breaths that escape while she sleeps, it's all so breathtaking. I don't want to sleep. I want to spend the rest of the night lying here, holding her, touching her, making her promises that she's not even aware of.

When I can no longer hold my eyes open, I drift off into a deep sleep. But even then, all I see behind my lids is her.

———

I WAKE in the morning and roll over, wanting to hold her, touch her, kiss her, but she's gone. Suddenly, I'm fully awake. The bathroom door is closed, so I wait several long minutes for her to come out. When I hear no signs of the water running, I get up and open the door to find the room empty. I quickly pull on a pair of boxers and go into the room across the hall, thinking maybe she's already up and getting dressed. But that room is empty too. Finally, I rush down the stairs, check the living room, dining room, and kitchen. She's not in any of them.

As a last resort, I go into my office and sit at my desk, pulling up the security footage. At three in the morning, she appears on the camera. She's walking down the dark driveway with her purse and her gym bag. Instantly, I know she's left me.

I pick up my phone and dial her number. It rings several times until it goes to voicemail.

"Damnit, Maddie," I curse, dialing her number again.

Seven more times I try calling, but all the calls are rejected. Finally, I slam the phone down and head back to my room to dress. It takes me only a few minutes to throw on a pair of jeans and a t-shirt. Within fifteen minutes of waking, I'm driving away from the house.

I'm stuck in morning traffic when my phone rings. I grab it and answer it without thinking, hoping it's Maddie, but my dad's voice rings out over the phone.

"Where are you?" he demands an answer.

"I won't be in today," I tell him, checking my watch to see that it's only five after nine. I want to laugh. I can't even be five minutes late without him calling and hassling me, but any amusement I may have gotten from this was taken away when she walked out on me this morning.

"What do you mean you won't be in today? We have a very important meeting."

"What meeting?" I ask, confused. I don't remember any meeting being on the schedule.

"The meeting we're having about approbate workplace behavior."

I roll my eyes. "Are you serious, Dad? I think everyone in the building knows what's going on. You think we need a meeting to catch everyone up?" My grip on the steering wheel tightens, causing my knuckles to turn white. *Why the fuck can't he leave it alone? Is he so controlling that he can't let me live my life without his input? Of course he is.*

"This is exactly what I've been warning you about, Bennet. Did you fire that woman?"

"No, she quit. But I have news for you; if she isn't welcome in your precious company, I'm not either."

"Bennet!" he yells.

"No, Dad. This isn't just about your company. This is about my life. I've finally found the woman I want to spend the rest of my life with. And you're not taking that away. I've let you take away every piece of what makes me me, but I won't let you take her. It's the both of us or neither of us." I hang up the phone without another word.

Traffic moves a few feet, and I hit the gas, too excited to wait any longer. My mind fills with images of last night: the way she held me close to her body, the sounds she made, the way she promised she'd love me for the rest of her life. She planned this. She knew it was our last night together. She knew what she was doing.

I know Maddie, and I know she was leaving in order to protect me. She thought I'd be better off alone, keeping my place at the company. But I don't want anything to do with that company. I want the dream I created with her by my side. The one where we lived in the suburbs with our children, working normal jobs, and getting to spend every single day together. That's what I want. And there's no way I'm going to let her walk away.

Finally, traffic starts moving, and I speed by as many cars as I can until I get off the highway and into her part of town. When I pull up to Damon's house, I wonder how I even got here safely. I don't remember a moment of driving since I got off the highway. All I saw was her. I pull up the parking brake and shut off the engine in one swift movement. I run from the car and to the front door, knocking over and over, but nobody answers.

I bend down and peek into the window. There's a small sliver that's not covered by the curtains, and I scan as much of the room as I can. The tv screen is black, and no lights are on. I look at my watch and realize that Damon and Jazz are probably at work. But where's Maddie?

A deep breath leaves my lungs in a rush as I crumble to the ground. I sit on the step, elbows resting on my knees and my head hanging. I don't know what to do. I don't know where to go to look for her. She has that check; she could be anywhere.

After minutes of sitting and feeling sorry for myself, I force myself to stand and walk back to my car. My immediate response is to drink, to drink and drink until I can no longer hold the glass, but I keep telling myself not to do that. I need to stay sober, just in case I do find her. I need to have a clear head to explain things to her, to make her see that I need her, not some stupid job that makes me feel like dying every day.

Instead of going home, I go to the gym. I don't pay attention to anyone or anything. I just go to the locker room where I know I have a spare set of clothes in my locker. After changing, I walk into the boxing ring with Phillip.

"Don't hold back today," I tell him, popping my neck and stretching my arms.

"You sure?" he asks as his brows raise, a little unsure.

I nod. "I need to feel some pain."

"Rough day?"

I laugh. "You could say that. Come on," I say, throwing a punch that he blocks.

I throw another hit, but he bobs and weaves until he's advancing on me. He swings, and even though I see it coming, I don't move. I stand still and take it. His fist lands on my jaw hard. It makes my ears ring, and my vision gets slightly blurry, but I shake it off and step toward him, swinging again. I land a hit to his chin just as he leans back to escape my punch. It didn't have much power, but I try again and again. I land several hits, and so does he. By the time we pull away, I have blood oozing out of my busted lip, and I can feel my jaw swelling.

"That's enough, man," Phillip says, leaning against the ropes to calm down.

"Thanks for kicking my ass," I say, stepping out of the ring.

He doesn't say anything as I walk to the locker room, but I feel his eyes on me the whole way. I strip out of my clothes and step into the shower to rinse off the sweat and blood. I hear the metal door open and slam closed.

"Are you going to tell me what's going on?" he asks loud enough for me to hear him over the water.

"She left," I reply.

"She wanted more, and you didn't?" he asks.

"No, we both wanted more, and we agreed to take it to the next level, to commit. But then my dad and the rest of the company found out. People were giving her shit, saying she only got the job because she was sleeping with me. My dad freaked out and is worried about the company image. He wanted me to fire her. So I basically quit, but she left so I could keep my stupid fucking job that I don't want anyway." I shut off the water and wrap a towel around my waist before stepping out to find him sitting on a bench.

"If you don't want the job, what's the problem?" he asks, raising his hands out to the side, palms facing upward.

"She won't answer her phone, and I don't know where she is." I shrug, letting my arms fall to my sides.

"So, find her, explain, and live happily ever after. What's so hard about that?"

I walk over to my locker and start pulling on my clothes. "I don't know, man. It's not that simple. I thought she'd stick by my side, you know? I don't want a woman that runs away as soon as something gets tough. She obviously didn't want to talk about it anyway. She got up and left while I was asleep last night." I pull on my shirt and slam my locker closed. "I'll catch ya later," I mumble, leaving the locker room. I'm tired, sore, and not in the mood to talk to anyone but Maddie. I hope Phillip doesn't take it personally. I've never been this way toward him. Right now, I feel Mr. Windsor coming on—the guy that's cold and harsh and doesn't want to hear shit from anybody.

I walk through the gym and am opening the door when someone bumps into me. I look down, and my eyes lock on icy blue.

"Maddie?" I whisper, surprised to be bumping into her. My heart starts to pound, and my lungs suddenly feel like they can't get enough oxygen.

Her eyes are wide with fear and her lips part. She shakes her head and turns to leave without a word.

"Hey!" I yell, but she keeps going.

"Madeline," I call after her again, but she still doesn't stop. I quickly jog up behind her and grab ahold of her wrist, spinning her around. When I look at her face, she has tears filling her eyes, and that causes me to freeze.

She looks at me, and I look at her, unable to move.

"Come with me," I plead in a whisper.

She shakes her head slightly. "I can't."

"Yes, you can. Let's talk. Explain this to me."

"Explain what, Bennet? That I slept with my boss and the whole company found out? I can't work there anymore. I refuse to go to that place every day and deal with the backlash of my mistake. But you, your name is on the building. You have to go." She jerks her hand away and starts back.

I follow after her. "I don't have to go, Maddie. I can do whatever I want. I want you, not that job."

She doesn't stop walking, and neither do I. "Maddie, you can't ignore me forever. I won't give up."

Finally, she stops and turns to face me. "Just let it go, Bennet. I won't be the reason your family disowns you. It won't work for us anyway. I'm going to find a new apartment, find a new job, and put all of this behind me. You should do the same. Go back to your office in the sky and taking home different women every night. Forget you met me."

"Goddamn it, Maddie. I love you," I yell.

Her eyes grow wide with fear and acknowledgment.

"I love you. I want to marry you. I want to have children with you. I don't want my old life. I want the one we created that day on the beach. If you can look me in the eye and tell me that you don't want that too, I'll let you walk away right now and never bother you again." My heart is pounding crazily in my chest. My stomach tightens with anticipation. Fear pumps through my body at an alarming rate. Is this it? Will she finally walk into my arms so we can fight this war together, or does she really want nothing to do with me?

Her blue eyes lock on mine, and she takes a deep, clearing breath. "I don't want that, Bennet. Now, please, just leave me alone."

She turns and leaves, and I can't do anything but watch her go. I can't call out to her. I can't reach out and touch her, make her feel me and my need for her to stay. I'm frozen in pain, in sadness, in anger.

I thought she was the one. I thought she was it for me. I guess something like that is impossible to know. But she made me feel so much more than any other person I've ever been with. Losing her, it's like losing the best part of myself. I don't know how I'll ever get over her, or if I ever will. Maybe I'm not meant to. Maybe Madeline Strickland was nothing more than a lesson. God's fucked-up way of telling me to keep living the life I had been up until I met her. Before her, I was dead set on staying single, enjoying my life and my money. All I wanted was someone to keep me company on lonely nights. I knew I should've kept my distance.

I turn and slowly walk back to my car. I slide behind the wheel and drive to my favorite restaurant. I have my usual medium-rare steak with a glass of scotch. As I sit at the table, waiting for my food, I look around at all the people near me. They're all smiling, laughing, carrying on conversations with the people they're with. They all seem like they have life figured out, like everything is simple and comes easy. I shake my head and scoff before finishing off my drink.

A waitress walks up to my table and places my plate in front of me. My vision is already doubling, and I can't help but look her up and down. She's wearing a knee-length black skirt, a white dress shirt, and a black-tie. Her long, dark hair is pulled into a sleek ponytail, and her blue eyes sparkle as her red lips turn up into a smile.

"Is there anything else I can get for you, sir?" Her tongue slides across her bottom lip, wetting it as her eyes take me in.

I pull out the chair next to me. "Why don't you join me for lunch?"

She quickly looks around. "I really shouldn't. I could get in trouble and lose my job."

I laugh and shake my head. "I assure you, you won't lose your job." I hold up my hand, and a waiter stops.

"Please, bring Ms….?" I look up at her.

"Stacy. Stacy Reddington." She sits in the chair.

"Please, bring Ms. Reddington whatever she wants and add it to my bill."

He nods before moving around the table to take her order. I pick up my fork and knife, slicing into my steak with a smile.

Maybe this won't be so bad after all.

MADDIE

"Okay, I'm here," Jazz says, walking into my new apartment.
"I'm in here," I call out from the bare living room.

She walks into the bright white room and freezes. "Man, you're lucky your co-worker needed someone to sublet this like yesterday. Haven't furnished yet, huh?"

I shake my head. "Yeah no kidding. Nope not yet."

She walks across the hardwood floor and sits next to me, leaning her back against the wall like I am. "Are you going to tell me what happened now?"

I take a deep breath, then pick up the bottle of wine, taking a long drink. "We broke up," I confess.

She inhales sharply. "What? Why?"

I shrug. "I just can't." I shake my head and another tear leaks from my eye. You'd think at this point, I wouldn't have anything left to cry.

She turns her body so that she's looking directly at me. "Madeline Michelle Strickland, spill it, every last detail. NOW!"

A giggle slips past my lips from hearing my full name. "Fine." I push myself up, pacing the floor. "Everything was going good. We'd been spending every day together, sleeping with one another, touching, kissing, flirting. I never had that freak-out moment, you know?

Like usually, I'd wake up the next morning and freak the fuck out because I'd fallen asleep and stayed the whole night. I'd break my neck trying to get out of there. But with Bennet, I didn't have anywhere to go. My apartment was gone. And he just made me feel so comfortable. We both agreed that we'd each have our own lives. But the more time I spent with him, the more I found myself falling for him. And then that stupid picture leaked, and everything went up in flames. I couldn't stand to look around the office because everyone was looking at me, whispering and giggling. And his dad," I roll my eyes. "He's pissed. He's afraid that it will tarnish his company or something. He told Bennet to fire me, to pay me off or shut me up somehow."

"What?" she asks, surprised.

I nod. "He wouldn't though. I told him he didn't have to because I quit. I mean, no way could I go back to working there after all this."

"Then what's the problem? He can keep his job, you can get a new one, and you guys can be together." She holds her hands in the air, palms facing the sky.

I shake my head as tears begin to fall freely. "I love him," I cry out.

She stands and rushes up to me, placing her hands on my biceps. "That's a good thing, Mads."

"We agreed to keep things simple, and then things started to change. He wants to get married. He wants kids." I sit back down on my pillow and pick up the bottle of wine.

She lets out a deep breath. "What's wrong with that?"

"Besides the fact that I've never in my life wanted marriage and kids?" I state the obvious. "He didn't ever want that either. He's saying this stuff to get me to stay. But I'm not going to give him something neither of us wants. I'm not going to be tied down, raising his kids only for him to realize in ten years that he never wanted that life. He will end up resenting me, probably cheating on me and leaving me with a life that I never wanted either." I lean my head against the wall and take another swig.

Jazz walks over and sits at my side. "So, what's the plan?"

I shrug. "I'm going to focus on me. I'm going to find a new job, furnish this place, and do what I was doing before I met him."

She snorts. "So, sleeping around? Never having any meaningful relationship? Being alone?"

I look up, and my eyes meet hers, but I can't answer her questions. Instead of talking, I resort to drinking my nasty wine.

After a long pause, she finally stands and heads for the door. "You know," she says, spinning around to face me. "All you're doing right now is pulling away because you're feeling something you've never felt before. You're scared. And that's fine. I was scared too. But you can't push this away. If you do, you'll regret it for the rest of your life. I've never known you to run away before. Don't start now, Maddie." Without another word, she turns and leaves.

When I hear the door click behind her, I set my bottle down and curl up into a ball on the floor. My eyes drift closed, and I pray that sleep takes me, but it doesn't. All I can see is him—his sparkling green eyes, his tan, toned biceps as he held me against the wall, the way his lips always curled up at the corners after he kissed me. I can feel his lips on mine, how soft and strong they were. I can smell his deep, rich scent.

Tears fill my eyes, finally flooding over and streaming down my cheeks. I know that Jazz is right; I shouldn't push this away. But I'm too afraid of the what-ifs. What if I do marry him? Will he end up hating me when he realizes that he never wanted marriage? What if I do have his children? Will we be happy? What if, in the end, we still end up breaking up? Will all the time between now and then be a total waste?

How do people do it? How can they just trust another person wholeheartedly? Trust them to love them forever, to support them, to be there through thick and thin, in the most important times? I've never met another person I could trust that much, not even Jazz. Jazz is my best friend, but even that doesn't mean that she'll always be able to be there for me. She's about to be a mom, and I know that baby will come before everything—as it should. But if I can't even trust her—a person I've known my whole life— to always be there, how can I trust a man I've just met?

Eventually, sleep finds me, and I give in, letting it take me to avoid facing the pain and confusion I feel.

———

WHEN I WAKE, I refuse to let myself think of anything but the task at hand. I shower, dress, and get ready for the day. When that's done, I lock up the apartment and head out, needing to buy basically everything for my apartment and look for a job.

I go to several stores and order the basic furniture I'll need: a couch, a bed, a couple tables, and lamps. Then, I head to Target to grab dishes, silverware, some towels, and necessities. After dropping everything off at home with the promise to myself that I'll put it up later, I head out for some coffee. While sitting at the table alone, I use my phone to find jobs and put in applications. My head is completely in the moment, only focusing on filling out my application, but then I get a whiff of familiar cologne, and my head jerks up, looking for Bennet. I scan every face around me, never finding him, only a man that's sitting directly behind me. I shake my head, wanting to clear it of the thoughts that have been threatening to cripple me all day. When thoughts of Bennet start popping in my head, I decide that it's time to get busy. I can't sit here any longer. I have to move, keep myself occupied. I slide my phone into my pocket and pick up my cup, heading for the door in a rush. I need the cool air to clear my head. I'm practically running when I bump into someone.

"Whoa," he says, reaching out and steadying me as I begin to topple backward.

I look up and find a good-looking man holding me. He has dark brown eyes, a dark scruff growing on his jaw, and his face is perfectly chiseled.

"I'm so sorry. I should probably slow down." I manage to stand upright, and he releases me.

"That's okay. I'm Tony." He holds out his hand.

I slide mine into his. "I'm Maddie."

He smiles, and my heart starts to pound. "Would you like to sit and have a cup of coffee with me?" He motions toward an empty table.

I look at him, the table, and back. I open my mouth to decline.

"On me," he tries. "I'll even throw in a muffin. You look like a blueberry girl."

I laugh and nod. "I am," I agree.

He smiles wide and holds his arm out in front of me. I turn and walk up to the counter with him following along behind me.

Tony and I sit next to the window, drinking our coffee, talking, and watching the day pass us by. When the sun starts to go down, he offers to keep our moment going by taking me out to dinner. Something inside of me wants to decline, but I force myself to go. Not only will it keep my mind off Bennet, but it's also free dinner.

As we walk down the busy street, he picks up where we left off. "So, you said you're between jobs?"

I nod. "I am. I was in data configuration at Windsor Wealth Management."

His eyes grow wide. "Wow. That's pretty impressive. Why'd you leave, if you don't mind me asking?"

I take a deep breath. "It wasn't the right work environment."

"I completely understand. I used to work for a big business like that. It's very stressful."

"Where do you work?" I ask, wanting to get the attention off me.

"This new place downtown called Striker Inc. And you know, now that you mention it, we're hiring a whole team of people. It's still a small company, but it's a good job. You should turn in an application."

I smile. "Thanks, I'll look into it."

We head into a Chinese restaurant and get seated. We both order, and as we talk about movies, music, and books, something inside of me feels weird. I don't want to be here. I want to force myself to get over Bennet, but at the same time, I don't want to forget how he made me feel. Being with him was exciting and fun; it was passion and adventure—I never knew where we'd end up. He opened my eyes to so many new things: boxing, racing, a world of privilege I didn't know anything about. And even though we weren't meant to get serious, he always showed respect for me and how much he cared.

I let out a deep sigh and pick up my glass of wine, swallowing it all in one gulp.

"I'm sorry," I tell him, standing. "I should probably go."

"Did I do something?" he asks.

"No, not at all," I say. "I just got out of a tough relationship, and this," I motion toward him, me, and the table, "it's just too much."

He nods. "I completely understand." He opens his wallet and tosses some cash on the table. "Let me walk you back."

"Really?" I ask. He's being so great about it all.

"Of course. I've been exactly where you are. Don't worry about this." He places his hand on my lower back and leads me from the restaurant.

Neither of us say anything as we walk back down the street toward the coffee shop. When we come to a stop in front of the building, he looks over at me. "Do you live far from here?"

I shake my head. "Just around the corner. Thank you for today. You were great."

"How long have you been broken up?" he asks, looking at me from beneath his lashes.

"Yesterday," I breathe out.

His eyes double in size. "Oh, wow. I thought you were going to say a couple months or something." He lets out a nervous laugh as he slides his hand into his jacket pocket, pulling out a card. "This is my number. I'm not saying you have to use it tomorrow or next month even, but I'd really like to get to know you better."

I reach out and take it. "Okay, thank you." I smile as I look down at the card that reads Stryker Inc. Tony Striker, CEO. I want to laugh. What are the chances I'd run into a good-looking guy, almost want to start something up with him, and have him be in a position of power? No way will I be filling out that application.

I slide the card into my pocket, and when I look up, he's leaning in. His hand cups my cheek, and his lips meet mine. I freeze, not knowing what to do. Should I kiss him back? I did have a good time with him today. Should I pull away?

My eyes flutter closed and try to feel something. I wait for the usual tingle that takes over, but there's nothing. Nothing but warm lips pressing against mine.

I place my hand on his chest and step back. "I'm sorry. I should go." Without another word, I rush past him, down to the end of the street, and around the corner. The second I'm no longer in his view, the sobs break free. It's now very obvious that I can't run from my feelings for Bennet. I can't make myself forget or ignore them. I can't trick myself into using those feelings for anyone else. There is no easy way of getting over someone you've fallen in love with. I think the only thing that will make things any different is time. I need to avoid men at all costs, focus on myself, and hopefully, as time passes, I'll love him a little less. Until the day comes that I have my old life back.

When I get up to my new apartment, I let myself in and go directly to the bathtub. I fill it full and sink into the warm water. I lean my head back and close my eyes. I have been refusing to think of him, but now, I welcome the thoughts. I think about training with him and watching the way his muscles flexed. I think about the time we went for a swim and ended up soaking wet in his bed. I think about secret meetings we had in his office. My body comes alive, burning with anticipation. Then, I think of that kiss with Tony. The way his soft lips touched mine, the way his tongue demanded entrance, and the way I felt nothing.

My eyes pop open. "Fuck," I cry out.

There's no denying that I'm in love with Bennet. The only question is: will I get over him? Do I want to? Will my life be better or worse without him?

Without a doubt, I know that not having him in my life will be the worst decision I could make. Starting something up with my boss wasn't my biggest mistake; leaving him alone in bed was. I am scared of what the future could have in store for us, but I'm even more afraid of always wondering instead of just finding out. Bennet is where my heart is. Bennet is my future.

I quickly jump out of the tub and race to put my clothes on. I grab my purse and keys and run down to the street where I hail a cab. The whole way over, I'm a nervous wreck. My heart is pounding, and my lungs are begging for oxygen. My legs won't hold still; they just bounce up and down the whole way. Finally, the cab pulls up to his house, and the gate is open. Instead of having the cab take me all the way to the door, I get out at the gate and hand over the cash.

On the walk up the drive, a million things fill my head. What if he's changed his mind? What if he doesn't want me anymore? What if I fucked up everything?

I walk up to the door and knock a few times, bouncing from foot to foot. Just when I'm about to turn around, the door opens. My eyes jump up, expecting to land on Bennet, but there's a woman instead. My first instinct is she must be a new maid, but she's not in uniform. She's wearing a pair of skin-tight jeans with black pumps. Her white t-shirt is ripped and torn, hanging off her shoulder and showing way too much cleavage. The shirt is tight and ends up above her bellybutton. Her dark hair, long and flowing around her, and her makeup is done perfectly.

Bennet must have done what I asked. He went back to his office in the sky and taking home different women every night. I'm glad to see that he doesn't waste time.

"Can I help you?" she asks.

I shake my head as I back away. "I'm sorry. Wrong house," I mumble, turning and running down the driveway. Tears fill my eyes until I can't see clearly. I fucked up. I got scared and pushed him away. I lost him. *I'm going to be alone forever, and it's all my fault.*

1 8

BENNET

I wake in the morning feeling like shit. My head is pounding, and my stomach is rolling. I think back on yesterday, remembering running into Maddie. I remember the way my heart broke when she said she didn't want me. I remember the emptiness I felt when she said those words. The last thing I remember was having lunch with that waitress, the way she openly flirted with me, and how every word she said was the exact opposite of what Maddie would say. Instead of being able to use her to replace Maddie, all she did was scream *I'm not Maddie*. I couldn't go forward with my plan. I paid for our lunch and left alone, deciding that I needed to come home where people couldn't see how big of a mess I was.

Based on the empty bottle of scotch in the bed beside me, my best guess is that I drank myself into a coma. I look at my watch and see that it's going on noon. I reach for my phone on the bedside table, but it isn't there. Probably for the best. I'm sure it's filled with missed calls from my father by now.

I force myself to stand and walk to the shower, only having to stop and empty my stomach once on the way. I collapse into the bottom of the shower and just sit there, letting the hot water wash over me. I can't think of anything but how shitty I feel and why I feel this way. I don't blame the scotch. I blame Maddie. She gave me something I never knew I needed. And then, she just ripped it away.

My head pounds and my stomach churns. My chest is filled with pain, and my head, my head is a mess of fucked up thoughts of what I should've done, should've said to stop her from leaving me. I lean my head back against the wall and let the heat soak into my body. I feel like I'm on fire between the hot water and the heat of my anger. I feel like I'm burning up from the inside out.

A part of me wants to be mad at Maddie. I try telling myself that she did this to me on purpose, that she used me. But deep down, I know that isn't true. Which emotion is better: heartbreak or anger? Either way, they're nothing compared to love and happiness—something I know I will never feel again.

When I finally manage to get myself off the shower floor, I pull on a pair of sweatpants and drape my towel around my shoulders while I go looking for my phone. I open my bedroom door and there it lies, screen shattered, in the hallway. Shards of thin glass pepper the hardwood floor around it. I grab it, and to my surprise, it turns on. I see fourteen missed calls from my mom, dad, and sister. But none from her. I swipe the screen and the picture before my eyes takes my breath away. It's a picture I snapped of Maddie from that night—the night she left me. Her eyes are closed, her lips in a pout. Her dark hair is fanned out around her.

I can tell that I was looking at this picture when I got pissed and smashed my phone. A pain slices through my heart, and I shake the loose glass from the phone before sliding into my pocket as I make my way down the stairs for coffee. As I'm pouring a cup, I hear my front door open and slam shut, causing me to jump and spill the coffee.

I spin around to see my sister, Val, running into the kitchen. She's breathless, and her eyes are wide. "Where the fuck have you been?"

"Here," I answer, turning back to my coffee.

"Why didn't you answer your phone?"

I pull it out of my pocket and slide it across the countertop. "Just found it," I say, taking a sip and grabbing a towel to soak up the mess I made.

I walk around the counter, intending on going into my home office, but she stops me.

"Bennet, Dad had a heart attack. He's in the hospital, and we don't know if he's going to make it," she says.

I stop dead in my tracks and turn around. "What? When?"

"He was in your office last night, alone. We don't know what time it happened, but your secretary found him this morning. We have to go to the hospital."

"Give me five minutes." I place the coffee on the counter and run to get dressed.

———

MY SISTER DRIVES us both to the hospital and leads me up to his room. The second we walk in, Mom stands and rushes up to me.

"Bennet," she breathes out, pulling me in for a hug. I hold her against my chest and let her cry into my shirt.

I smooth her hair back, trying to be here for her at this moment, but my eyes are locked on my dad's lifeless body. He looks ten years older just lying there, eyes closed. The harsh lighting illuminates his face, making his fine lines and wrinkles more prominent. His cheeks seem hollow, and his skin looks dewy and pale.

"What have the doctors had to say?" I ask, voice straining to hold back the tears. Seeing him this way, I don't see the man that was yelling at me just the day before. I see the man that used to take me for ice cream every Sunday. The guy that taught me about classic cars. The guy that started my love for racing and boxing.

Mom shakes her head as she pulls away. "They're still running tests." She grabs a tissue and dries her eyes.

"Has he woken up at all?" I ask.

"He's in and out, but never for long," Val says from behind me. "Mom, why don't I take you to get cleaned up, maybe get something to eat?"

"No, I have to stay here. What if he wakes up again?" Her fragile hands are shaking as she pushes her red hair away from her face.

"Bennet will stay, Mom. Come on; you need a break," she insists.

"Yes, Mom. Please, go take care of yourself. I won't go anywhere," I promise her.

Reluctantly, she nods, and my sister leads her from the room.

I take the empty seat she just left, and I make myself comfortable.

The room is silent. All I can hear is his deep, even breathing, and the low hum of the machines he's hooked to. My stomach is still upset and rolling, gurgling, and making me feel sick. I hate that I let my emotions get the best of me yesterday. My father was doing my job; he was in my office. If I'd just acted like an adult and went to work, none of this would've happened. Only God knows how long he laid there. He'd always been one to put in extra hours, but he never stayed past midnight. And Sarah doesn't come in until eight. He could've been laying in that floor in pain for eight or more hours.

I pull my broken phone from my pocket and go through the call log. I have a missed call from him at five yesterday, another at nine, another at ten, and then the last one at twelve-thirty. He could've been calling me for help, and I didn't help him because I was drunk and hurt.

Maybe he's always been right about me. I care for nobody but myself. I'm selfish and act like a child instead of a man.

"Bennet," I hear Dad whisper low.

I jump from hearing his voice, and I spring forward, needing to be closer to hear what he has to say.

"Dad? I'm here," I tell him, grabbing his hand.

"Ben, I'm sorry," he says, out of breath and sounding hoarse.

I shake my head as my eyes fill with tears. "Sorry? What for?"

"I should've trusted you. I shouldn't have—"

"No, shhh, you don't have to say this. Just rest."

He shakes his head slightly. "The company is yours. It was always meant to be yours. I made myself sick because I couldn't let it go and trust you." He pauses to catch his breath, and even though he's saying everything I've ever wanted to hear, I don't want to hear it now. Not this way.

"Everything you've done in life, it's all turned to gold. I shouldn't have started second-guessing you. I'm stepping back. I want you to run it as you see fit."

"Thanks, Dad. But we can talk about all this later. Right now, you need rest."

He clutches his heart and his muscles tense. A loud beeping sound goes off.

I stand. "Are you okay? Let me get your doctor."

But he doesn't release me. Instead, he squeezes tighter. "You're the man of the family now, Ben. Take care of your mother and sister."

"Dad? No! Let me get help." I tug my hand out of his and run to the door. I throw it open and jump out into the hall. "I need a doctor!" I yell, spinning in a circle, looking in every direction. Mom and Val just rounded the corner, and they both have concerned looks on their faces as they run my way.

A nurse with a doctor on her heels runs into the room.

"What's happening?" Val asks.

Tears flood my eyes and fall over my cheeks. "I think he's having another heart attack," I cry out, pointing to the room.

Mom runs into the room with Val behind her. But I can't go in there. I can't stand to see him sick and weak and in pain. I turn my back on them and lean against the windows, looking out over the city that's still moving at the speed of light. The world is going on, just as it should. It doesn't know the man I've always respected, loved, feared, and sometimes hated, is slipping away. The world doesn't know the hole he's going to leave when he's finally gone.

If possible, my heart feels like it splits open and I collapse into the floor, landing on my knees. I put my back to the wall, drawing my knees up and letting my elbows rest of them as I hang my head. It feels like an eternity of waiting, but I hear my mother scream, and a crashing noise fills my ears.

"Mom!" Val yells, and that gets me up and running back into that room.

I see the doctor pull the sheet up over my dad's head, and then look to find my mother on the floor, crying while my sister holds her, medical equipment surrounding them. My whole world breaks and I can't do anything but watch as everything unfolds.

———

VAL and I get Mom home and tucked into bed. We stay until she's cried herself to sleep. Val promises to return after she's taken me home, even though Mom won't know the difference. She took a powerful sleeping pill before we tucked her in.

On the drive home, neither of us say much. Finally, she breaks her silence. "What's been going on with you? Mom said you haven't been going to work. You were hungover as fuck this morning, and you don't look the best."

I wave her off.

"Bennet, tell me what's going on. We've all had a lot on our plates today. Can we just talk about whatever it is so I can stop thinking about Dad?"

I let out a long breath. "I fell in love," I confess.

She inhales sharply. "What? With who? And how did that happen?" The last question was a joke, but neither of us laughs. We don't have it in us.

"I met a girl at the gym. Something about her, she just called to me. I couldn't get her out of my head. And then, I discovered she worked at the company." I lean my head back. "She didn't want to move forward because I was her boss. But I knew that we were meant to be. I wouldn't let her go. Finally, I wore her down, and we agreed to keep things casual. But casual got thrown out the window. We couldn't help but fall for one another. Just when we decided to commit, the stupid newsletter at work went out, and a picture of us together was in it. Everyone found out, Dad had a fit and demanded that I fire her. I told him no and that I'd rather quit than fire her, which is why I haven't been going to the office. And when I told her I wanted her, not the job, she refused. She pushed me away. That's why I got shit-faced last night. I'm trying to get over her."

She shoots me a grin. "Sounds like she's the one."

I nod. "She's the only one I ever even thought about marrying and starting a future with. But…" I shake my head.

Val pulls into my driveway, and we both climb out of the car. "Let's get a drink," she says, opening the door and walking in.

I lead her to my office and pour us both a stiff drink.

"Give it time," she says.

"Give what time? Time to get over her?"

"No, moron. Time for you both to realize that what you two have can't be ended."

I sit behind my desk. "I don't know. She… she doesn't want anything to do with me, Val. I don't know how I can make her listen to me, listen to herself. I know she loves me. I know she does, but I think that scares her."

Someone begins knocking on the door, and I throw my head back, letting out a long breath, not happy about being bothered.

Val sets her drink down. "I'll answer the door." She walks out of the office and toward the front door.

"Can I help you?" I hear her ask.

But then I hear nothing.

A few seconds later, she walks back into the office.

"Who was it?" I ask.

She shrugs and picks up her glass again, moving across the room to fill it. "I don't know. She saw me and took off."

I feel my brows draw together in confusion. "How'd she get in?" I ask, mostly to myself as I turn to face the computer.

"We didn't close the gate," Val says, moving behind my desk to look at the computer screen as I rewind the surveillance footage.

Before my eyes, in black and white, is Maddie. I stand so quickly, it causes Val to step back suddenly.

"That's her," I nearly yell, pointing at the screen.

"That's her? The one?" she asks, eyes widening.

I nod, unable to tear my eyes from the screen as I watch her spin around and run back down the driveway.

"Well, what the hell are you doing in here? Go after her!" She pushes me toward the door.

"But what about you? Mom?"

"Mom's toasted right now and sound asleep. Just go! Go get her!" She waves me off, chasing me out of the office and toward the door.

"What do I say?" I ask, turning to face her while walking backward to the door.

"Anything. Just go before she gets away." With one final shove, I'm outside, and she's slamming the door in my face.

I look toward the road, even though I can't see anything but my yard and the brick wall surrounding it. Without even thinking of what I'll say if I find her, I take off in a sprint, running for the gate. I run down the driveway, through the gate, and to the street. I stop, looking to my right and left, but she's gone. How could she have gotten away so fast? Maybe she had a cab waiting for her? Maybe she's walking and just rounded the corner.

I run back up the drive and get behind the wheel of Val's car. I speed from the house, driving in every direction, but I never find her. She's gone. Probably gone forever, thinking that Val is just some random girl I brought home for the night.

I hit the steering wheel and curse loudly.

When I get back home, Val takes off, and I go directly to my office. I pour another drink and dial her phone over and over.

But she never answers.

MADDIE

MADDIE
THREE MONTHS LATER…

"THE APARTMENT LOOKS AMAZING," Jazz says, walking back into the living room, holding her swollen belly.

"Yeah, it looks great," Damon says. "That new job must be paying you pretty well to decorate like this."

I smile and nod. "Yeah, at Chance Security, I'm making twice what I was making at Windsor." I pour two glasses of wine and hand one over to Damon. "Jazz, there's sparkling water in the fridge. Can you grab it for me?"

She hands it over, and I pour a champagne glass for her.

"I'm glad you called, Mads. It looks like you're doing really well. I'm not going to lie; we've been worried about you," Jazz says, standing across from me.

"And the next time you change your number, you better give it to me, you little brat. I thought you fell off of the face of the planet," Damon adds on.

I laugh. "I'm sorry. I gave it to Jazz. I just assumed that she'd passed it along."

We all hold up our glasses. "To your brand-new, beautiful apartment," Jazz says as we all clink glasses.

"And to you finally moving into your new home," I add before taking a sip. "How are you liking being out of the city?"

We all move toward the living room to sit down. "It's so nice," Jazz says. "It's quiet, and the sky is so clear. I love sitting out by the pool and being able to see the stars. And I can't wait until I can get into that hot tub."

Damon nudges her. "Yeah, we have some memories to rewrite in that hot tub." He grins and winks.

I remember Jazz telling me about how Damon took her back to our childhood house to rewrite the memories of us growing up. I guess that's one they haven't gotten to yet.

Jazz jabs her elbow into his ribs and turns to look at me. "So, what's the plans for your future, Mads? Other than being the best aunt this baby could have." She smiles and rubs her growing belly.

I smile, happy that she's sweet-talking me. "I don't know for sure. I mean, I'm done with my apartment. I love my job, and I'm making a ton of money." I shrug. "I guess I'm just going to keep living. I do have a date tonight though. And no, before you ask, I don't work with him."

They laugh. "Have you heard from Bennet?" Damon asks, and it feels like the whole room has shifted.

I shake my head. "Nope, he doesn't know where I live, and I changed my number for a reason. That night I went to his house, he had another woman there. He called me over and over, but I didn't answer. I figured, if he's going to do what I told him to do, I should too. I said I was going to move on and forget, and that's exactly what I'm doing."

Jazz looks over at Damon. "How's he doing anyway? You haven't said anything about him in a while."

Damon nods, and I can't help but focus on every word he says. "He's doing okay. After his dad passed, it took a while to get everything in order. But he's running the company like always, and he works in his spare time building his drag cars."

My eyes grow wide. "His dad died?"

He nods. "Yeah, it was really hard on him. He missed a ton of work, and every time I called to check on him, he was plastered. But he pulled himself out of it, came back to work, started this new business on the side, and I think he's finally starting to date again."

My eyes fall to the table between us, and I bite my bottom lip. My heart is racing from hearing about Bennet, and there's this sensation in my stomach that makes me feel uneasy and a little sick. My mind begins drifting off, thinking about the time we spent together. I can't even count how many times I cried myself to sleep after going to his house that night. Suddenly, I regret changing my number. Maybe I should've heard him out. Deep in my heart, I know I still belong to him, no matter how many guys I date or hook-up with to fight off the feelings.

But I'm glad that he's moved on and is doing well. It sounds like he's doing better than I am. I still think of him often, and a few times, I've dialed his number just to hear his voice. I never talked though, and he stopped calling my number back after the first dozen times.

I miss him. Everything in me misses him: the way he would look at me, the way he'd touch me, the way everything in the world felt right when we were together. I miss his scent, his laugh, the sound of his voice. I miss the heat that would radiate off of him when we'd sleep. I even miss the soft snores that would escape after we spent hours having sex.

"What time is your date?" Jazz asks, snapping me from my thoughts.

"Oh, um, eight," I answer, mindlessly.

"You know it's going on seven now, right?"

My head pops up, and my eyes land on the clock on the wall. "Fuck. I have to get ready." I set down my glass and sprint down the hall toward my room.

I hear them laughing from behind me.

"Call me tomorrow, Mads. Let me know how it goes."

"I will. Thanks for coming. Maybe this weekend I'll drive out and check out all the work you've done to the old house," I yell down the hallway as I pull my black dress up over my body.

"Love you," they both say in unison.

"Love you back," I yell, rushing to the vanity to fix my hair and makeup.

It's pushing eight when I step back and look myself over. My black dress hugs every curve and ends mid-thigh. My black pumps make my legs look longer and shapelier. And my dark hair is soft and flowing around in me. I add a little red lipstick to my lips and grab my clutch just as someone knocks on the door.

I quickly pull it open to find James on the other side. I smile and lean in for a quick kiss. "Hi," I say when I pull away and close the door behind me.

"You look beautiful," he breathes out, handing over flowers.

"Thank you." I take the flowers and set them inside before stepping back out and locking the door.

"This is a nice building. Have you lived here long?"

"Just over three months now. My last place caught on fire. Luckily, I had insurance, or I never would've had the money to afford this place."

"Sometimes things end for a better future," he says, and for some reason, I can't help but read into that statement. Maybe things ended with Bennet to pave the way for him. Maybe Bennet wasn't supposed to be my happily ever after. Maybe Bennet was only placed in my life so I'd recognize love when it came around. I wish I could believe in fate, but Bennet hasn't been placed in front of me since. If we were meant to be together, fate wouldn't take so long, would it?

I shake my head. "My thoughts exactly," I agree, wrapping my hand around his arm as we step into the elevator.

He leads me outside and opens the door to a fancy sports car.

"Is this yours?" I ask.

He nods. "Did you picture me having something else?"

I laugh. "No, this looks just like you," I say, sliding into the seat. As he walks around the car to get behind the wheel, I can't help but think of Bennet again and the first time I got into his car. *God, why is he on my mind so much tonight? It must be because Jazz and Damon mentioned him. It doesn't mean anything.* I take a deep breath and clear my head, wanting to focus on James and give him a fair shot since this is my first attempt of dating since Bennet.

"So, where are we going?" I ask as he shifts into drive.

"I figured we'd have a nice dinner, and then maybe go somewhere for drinks?"

I nod. "Sounds like a plan."

We have a fancy dinner at some expensive place, the kind of dinner that looks beautiful but doesn't come close to filling you up. When we leave, I almost ask to run through a drive-through before going for drinks, but I don't. When we pull up to some club I've never been to, he climbs out and hands over the keys to the valet. I open my door just in time for him to catch it and help me out of the car. The red rope is removed, and we're allowed to walk into the building. I think we're heading to the bar, but he directs me to a flight of stairs and into a private VIP area. There's a quiet room that's lit up with black lights. It only has a couch and one table with a fully stocked bar. He sits me down and then heads to our private bar for our drinks.

The way the space is set up, one wall is nothing but windows, overlooking the rest of the club. I stand and walk up to the window, looking down at the bar and crowded dance floor. My eyes skim the room, and for some reason, they're drawn over to the far corner where there's a man standing up from his table, eyes locked on mine.

It's Bennet.

Even though it's dark and hard to see since it's so far away, deep in my soul, I know who's looking at me. My lungs and heart freeze and my lips part as I stand there staring back at him.

James walks up to me and hands me my drink, snapping me from my daze.

"So, what do you think? Have you ever been here before?"

I take a sip, hoping it clears the fog from my head. "No, it's a little crazy, isn't it? I mean, who goes to a club to be alone?" I ask, motioning toward the empty VIP section we're in.

He shrugs. "I like to come here. I can have my private room to relax in, then head down to the club if I feel like socializing. But right now, I want to get to know you better." He takes my hand and pulls me back to the couch.

We both place our drinks on the glass table in front of us, and he turns his body toward mine, his hand landing on my knee. "So, tell me, Madeline, what is it you like to do outside of work?"

I shrug. "What everyone else does, I guess. Usually, through the week, I just hang out at home and have a quiet dinner, or I'll go to the new gym I joined. On the weekends, I get all my running done, and I'll hang out with my best friend. You know, pretty normal stuff."

"You work out? I figured you did. Not many women have an ass like yours." He grins and winks.

I fake a smile, not sure if that's supposed to be a compliment or not.

He picks up his drink and finishes it off before standing for another. It seems, the more he drinks, the less he cares about what he says. I've known him for a month now, and he's always been rather shy and quiet. When he did flirt, it was always something sweet. It wasn't talking about my ass and placing his hands on my body. I try to count how many drinks he's had tonight and figure it has to be at least six between dinner and now.

He sits back at my side and his hand lands back on my leg, but this time, higher up on my thigh.

"You are amazing, you know that?" he whispers, leaning in and pressing his mouth to mine. I kiss him back for a moment but then lean away, breaking the kiss. "God, you taste like heaven," he whispers, moving back in.

I place my hand on his chest, hoping he understands it means that this is far enough. I don't mind a simple kiss, but I'm not going to be fucking him in front of this bartender either. His kiss gets harder and more forced. Before I know it, his body is almost completely on top of mine, and I'm being pushed back against the arm of the couch. I break my lips away from his.

"James, that's enough," I say, just as he moves his mouth back to mine. His hand comes up and squeezes my breast, and I push him off of me, causing him to fall into the floor.

"Don't ever call me again," I say, grabbing my clutch and storming out of the room.

I slam the door behind me, but I can feel him chasing after me. I pick up the pace but can't go too quick on the stairs in these heels. My eyes flash over to the corner, where I see Bennet stand up when his eyes land on mine, but I tear them away in an effort to keep my head down so that I don't fall.

I push my way through the crowd, and just as I'm almost to the door, James reaches out and grabs my wrist. He spins me around to face him. "Maddie, what's your problem?" he asks loudly, above the music.

"Let me go, James." I try pushing his hands off me.

"No, just tell me what's wrong," he tries, his hands growing tighter around my wrists.

Bennet steps up to my side, only looking at James. His jaw is twitching, and even though he looks cool and collected, I can tell he's ready to pounce. "Let her go," he demands.

"Who the fuck are you?" James asks, turning his attention back to me. "Come on, Maddie. Just come back upstairs with me," he pleads.

"I said let her go." Bennet steps forward, shoving James back, and catching me when I stumble.

The moment his hands are on my body, I feel like I've been set on fire. Our eyes lock, and I see his Adam's apple bob as his jaw tenses.

Our connection is cut short though because James jumps between us, shoving Bennet back.

"I don't think you want to do this, man," Bennet tells him.

James nods. "You inserted yourself into our business. I suggest you walk away and leave us alone."

Bennet shakes his head. "I can't do that."

James shrugs and begins rolling up his sleeves. "Your funeral." He jumps toward Bennet and Bennet reacts quickly, swinging and landing a solid hit to James' stomach. He recovers quickly and swings, landing a blow to Bennet's jaw. I hear the loud crack over the music, but it doesn't faze him. He doesn't even stumble back. He just attacks, throwing punch after punch and not stopping until James is running away with a busted lip and a bruised eye that's swelling shut.

I'm standing by the bar, frozen, while the whole club is going crazy. I hear someone yell that the police are coming; bouncers are going crazy, now trying to break up all the fights that started. But all I see is Bennet. He holds out his hand, and I look from his hand to his eyes and back.

"Come with me, Maddie," he asks, low so only I can hear.

I hear a gunshot from somewhere in the room, and I jump, slapping my hand into his. He pulls me into the street and inside his waiting limo. He slams the door closed behind us and yells for the driver to go. The driver hits the gas so fast, it throws us both back in our seats, tires squealing.

Neither of us talks for a moment; we just let our hearts calm and even out. Finally, he looks over at me in the darkness. I look over at him, unsure of what to say. His jaw ticks and his Adam's apple bobs again. He opens his mouth to say something, but I can't wait to find out what it is. In fact, I don't care what he's about to say. I just lean forward and press my mouth to his.

BENNET

I want to yell and scream at her for even going out with that guy. I want to tell her that I better never find her again with a guy like that, but I don't have time to say any of it. She leans forward and presses her mouth to mine, and my whole fucking world stops. There's nothing left but me and her. My hands reach out and pull her onto my lap as I deepen the kiss. She tastes of a sweetness I've missed. My blood begins to boil beneath my skin, and my heart is pounding like a jackhammer. Even though there are so many things to talk about, I can't get myself to break this kiss to say any of it. All I can do is live in this moment, hoping it never ends.

Her hips start to move back and forth against me, causing my dick to harden like stone. Her hands start pushing my jacket off my shoulders, and I quickly shrug out of it. I break the kiss.

"What's your address?" I whisper.

She rattles it off, and just as I yell it up to the driver, her mouth is back on mine, her hands, loosening my tie. I trail my lips over to her jaw and down her neck. She lets out a moan that makes me feel like I've been struck by lightning; it makes my dick twitch against her.

"We're here," she says, sliding off my lap. She takes my hand and pulls me from the car and into the building. She leads me to the elevator and pushes a button. When the doors close, I'm back on her. My hands tour her body, needing to feel every inch, needing to make sure this is real and not some stupid dream—God knows I've had many of these dreams over the several months.

Her fingers get to work on the buttons on my shirt, unbuttoning them at the speed of light. I pick her up and press her against the wall, pulling back enough to look into her icy blue eyes.

Just looking in those eyes brings up so much emotion for me. I'm drowning in it: sadness, pain, regret, and love. "Fuck, I've missed you so much," I whisper as I move my lips back to hers. My hand slides up her inner thigh, brushing against her bare core. Without warning, I slide my finger deep inside, making her call out loudly.

A part of me wants to be pissed that she decided against the panties tonight for that asshole she was with, but the rest of me just wants to pretend that she knew she'd run into me.

The elevator dings and the doors open. She breaks our kiss, and I allow her to slide down the wall. I pull away, but she doesn't release my hand—like if she does, I'll disappear. She drags me from the elevator and up to a door. While she digs around for her keys, I press my groin against her ass so she can feel how turned on I am. My hands pull her hair away from her neck, and my lips find the soft skin beneath it.

She gets the door open and we stumble through. She spins around, catching my lips with hers. She pushes my shirt over my shoulders and onto the floor. When her hands land on my belt buckle, I pull away.

"I don't know what this is, but I don't care." I spin her around and place her hands on the table in front of her. My fingers find the zipper on her dress, and I slowly lower it. "I've spent the last several months dreaming of this day, Maddie. And now that it's here, I'm taking my time with you. This won't be hurried or rushed." I pull her dress down her body until it lands in a puddle at her feet. When I glance down at her, she's completely naked, wearing nothing but those fucking black pumps. "I'm going to fuck you until you beg me to stop." I reach around and slide my fingers between her folds as I gently bite down on her shoulder. "When I'm done with you, Maddie, you won't be able to walk away from me again." I spin her around and catch her lips with mine. My tongue demands entrance, and she allows it as she wraps herself around my body.

I place my hands on her ass as I carry her through the apartment until I find her bedroom, and then I drop her onto the bed. As she scoots up the bed, I unbutton my pants and kick them off, watching her the whole time as she lays herself back and watches me. She's more toned than ever. It's easy to see she's been keeping up with her workouts even though I haven't left the gym in hopes of finding her. I take her ankle in my hand and unstrap her shoe. When I toss it to the side, I do the same with the other. I place her first foot to the left of me, and then the other to the right, so she's spread out for me. She doesn't shy away. She licks her lips and lets out a soft moan when I pick up her knee and press a kiss to the inside.

When my lips kiss up her right leg, I pick up the other and do the same. Finally, I kiss my way to her center, and I suck her clit into my hot mouth. Being able to taste her again has me ready to explode. She's breathing heavy and moaning and whimpering. When my name slips past her lips, I have no choice but to slide into her. She wraps her arms around my neck as I thrust into her as hard as I can.

"Fuck, I missed you," I whisper against her mouth while I roll my hips against her.

"I'm sorry, Bennet," she cries out. "I love you," she whispers, causing my hips to pause. My hands cup her face, and our eyes lock; hers are full of tears.

"I didn't want to mess things up for you; that's what I told myself. But honestly, I was scared. I was scared of the feelings I was having for you. And I was scared when you said you wanted marriage and kids." The tears overfill her eyes now.

I shake my head. "I just want you, Maddie. The rest of it, I don't care about. I just want you, baby. I need you," I confess, moving my lips to hers where I kiss her softly for the first time in months. Her muscles squeeze my cock that's still inside her, and my hips start to move gently on their own.

"I love you, Bennet," she mumbles against my lips.

"I love you too, Maddie," I say, never allowing my hips to stop.

It feels like her muscles are squeezing every inch of my cock, and it makes my release rise to the surface. I know I'm about to come and I can't stop it. I place my hand between us and rub her clit while I thrust up into her. Just as her cries and whimpers find my ears, my release bubbles over. I let out a loud moan as my hips take on a mind of their own, moving back and forth quickly with shaky jerks. We ride out our release together until we're both spent from the physical and emotional toll on our bodies.

I remove myself from her and pull her to my chest, my fist tangling in her hair and pulling her mouth back to mine.

"Please, don't ever leave me again," I beg between passionate kisses.

She shakes her head. "I'll never be able to walk away." She lays her head on my bicep, and her blue eyes lock on mine. "I wasn't able to fully walk away that day. Even though I left, I left every part of me with you. Finding that woman at your house..." Her sentence breaks off.

"That was my sister. She had brought me home from the hospital after my dad passed away."

She nods. "Damon told me about his death. I was just so..." she shakes her head.

I pull her closer. "Tell me what was going on in your head," I plead.

She places her fist under her head and looks at me. "First, I was scared because you meant more to me than anyone ever has, you know? I mean, we were just supposed to be casual, and then things got out of hand so quickly between us. I was scared that you'd end up sick of me and breaking my heart."

"So, you decided to break your own heart by leaving me?" I ask, not understanding entirely.

She softly laughs. "I knew it would hurt to leave, but I thought if I felt that strongly about you after such a short time, being with you longer would only hurt worse. And then the stuff with the company and your dad, I just didn't want to be the thing that broke your family."

"And after I told you I didn't care about the job?"

She nods. "Then I was afraid of what you were saying about wanting marriage and kids with me. For one, I never wanted marriage and kids, period. And two, I was worried that if we eventually did end up married with kids, you'd one day wake up and realize that you had a life you never wanted. That you'd end up resenting me and divorcing me or something. I know it all sounds crazy, but—"

"That's what love does. It makes you think and overthink. It can drive you crazy if you let it." I press a kiss gently to her forehead.

She lets out a deep breath, exhaling all the stress, sadness, anger: all of it that's been building over the time we've been apart.

"So, who was this dip-shit you went out with tonight?"

She laughs. "His name is James. I met him not too long after we broke up. I always go outside on my lunch break, and he's always there, sitting at the fountain. He works in the building across the street from mine. What about you? Have you gone on any dates?"

"I was on one tonight."

"You were? And you just left her there?" she asks, still tangled up with me.

I laugh. "Yeah, but she wasn't alone. She has a whole group of friends to get her home safely."

She shakes her head. "We're a mess, you know it?"

I hug her closer. "Yeah, but I don't want to be a mess with anyone else."

"Me either. I really am sorry for freaking out and running on you. It won't happen again," she assures me with her hand on my cheek.

"It better not," I tease, rolling us over so that I land perfectly between her legs. My body begins to come alive just from knowing I'm where I want to be, where I should be.

"Hey, Damon said you opened another business?"

"I did. I bought some property outside of the city, in the suburbs. Right now, it's just a big lot with a pond and a pole barn. But I'm already drawing up plans for a house."

Her brows raise. "A house, huh?"

I nod. "I want a country house. Someplace quiet where we can unwind."

"We?" she asks.

I laugh, unaware that I said *we*. "If you want to, I mean. I'm not making plans for our future without you. Either way, I figured I needed a place for my business, and property is always a smart investment."

She smiles wide. "I love that idea."

"You do?"

She nods. "I don't know where we'll be in the future, Bennet. I don't know if we'll get married. I don't know if I'll ever want kids. But I do know one thing."

"What's that?"

"I will be by your side, no matter where you go."

I can't hold back the smile that sentence brings on. I lean forward and kiss her deeply, wanting to make sure I express how happy I am that we're finally in the same mind space.

She presses against my chest, and I pull away, confused.

"Join me for a shower?" she asks, sliding out from underneath me.

"I'd love to." I smack her playfully on the ass as I chase her to the bathroom. She squeals and laughs as she dodges my hands. But finally, I catch her, pick her up against me, and step into the shower. With her back against the wall and the water beating down on us, I slide into my rightful place.

———

"Mads, where are ya?" Damon yells, walking into the apartment.

My eyes pop open, and so do Maddie's.

"Maddie!" Damon yells again, and based on the sound of his voice, he's getting closer to the bedroom.

We both jump up and start pulling on clothes.

"Should I hide?" I whisper, pulling on whatever clothes I can find.

She shakes her head. "No, we have to tell him eventually."

He knocks on the bedroom door just as she pulls my shirt over her head. "Maddie?" he asks through the door.

"Come in," she calls out, giving me a sidelong glance. I look down to find myself in her oversized gray sweatpants. The ones that say Juicy across the ass in bright pink. I'm about to rip the seams, and I'm sure she'll be pissed if I hulk out in them.

The door opens and Damon walks in. "Hey, there you are," he says before his eyes land on me. "What's he doing here?" he asks, looking at me but talking to Maddie.

She walks over to me and wraps her arm around my stomach. "We ran into one another last night."

"I thought you had a date last night?" he asks, placing his hands on his hips.

She lets out a laugh. "You're really getting this *dad* thing down, aren't you?"

I want to laugh, but I hold it back. Just looking at the way he's standing screams disappointed father.

His eyebrow lifts, not amused.

"My date turned into a sleaze ball fast."

"What's that mean?"

"It means he got a little handsy and tried to stop me from walking out of the club. Bennet stopped him."

I snort and roll my eyes. "And I'm sure I'll have court papers on my desk on Monday too. No doubt he'll press charges."

Damon's eyes grow wide. "You kicked his ass? In the club?"

I nod as my hand comes up to massage my temples. Already, I'm getting a headache just from thinking about it.

"Dude, why are you wearing my sister's pants?" Damon asks.

I look down at my pants and shrug. "You know me," is all I can say.

Damon smiles. "Well, to be honest, I'm glad you guys are back together. I saw you together, and I saw you when you were apart, and you were both a mess. Maybe things can get back to normal around here, huh?"

We all agree, and Damon pulls us both in for a hug. "But what I told ya before, it still stands."

Maddie looks up at me. "What did he tell ya?"

"That if I broke your heart, he'd kick my ass."

Even she laughs, knowing that Damon could never kick my ass.

"Jazz is in the kitchen. We brought over breakfast. Get dressed and join us. We have some good news." Damon quickly leaves the room.

I let out a deep breath. "I'm glad he didn't try kicking my ass. I would've hated having to beat him up in front of his little sister."

She laughs. "Just don't tell him that."

We both dress in our own clothing and walk out of the bedroom and into the kitchen. Jazz is setting plates for six.

"Hey, juicy," Damon teases when he sees me.

I hold up my middle finger.

"Who else is coming?" Maddie asks.

"Mom and Dad," Damon says. "I didn't realize that Bennet was here, but now's as good of a time as any to introduce them. Don't you think?" He grins as he wraps his arm around Jazz.

She finally looks up, and her eyes grow wide. "Oh, my God. Are you two back together?" she asks in a high pitched voice that hurts my ears.

I wrap my arm around Maddie's shoulders and pull her to my side while we both smile and nod.

Jazz screams with excitement and rushes over to give us both a hug. When she pulls away, she has tears running down her face.

"What's wrong?" I ask, handing her a napkin.

"I'm just so happy!" She cries even louder.

Damon walks over and pulls her in for a hug. "Pregnancy hormones," he points out.

Maddie and I both nod but then quickly back away. I pull her off to the side. "Is that what happens when women get pregnant?" I ask in a whisper, afraid of Jazz hearing.

"That and many more things," she replies.

I press my lips together. "I think I'll leave the kids decision up to you. I'm not going to lie; crying women freak me out."

She laughs and smacks me against the chest. "Why?"

"I don't know. I just don't ever know what to say. I mean, is there a right thing to say?"

"In her case, not really. You just gotta let her know you understand, even if you don't." She leans in and kisses me quickly, just as someone knocks on the door.

Maddie pulls away and rushes toward the door. "Hey, Mom, Dad," she greets them both with a hug.

Damon hugs his mom and shakes his dad's hand, and then Jazz gives them both a hug. When they're all done greeting one another, everyone looks at me.

I force a smile onto my face but am at a loss for words. I feel frozen while everyone looks at me like they expect me to break out in song or something. Finally, after Maddie watches me squirm for a little while, she steps up.

MADDIE

"Mom, Dad, this is Bennet Windsor, my boyfriend," I say, moving over to Bennet's side.

"Did you say boyfriend?" my mom asks.

I laugh and nod. "I did."

Mom smiles wide as she walks over. "She's never called anyone her boyfriend before. You must be quite special," she says, pulling Bennet in for a hug he has no say over.

Bennet laughs and hugs her gently. When Mom pulls away, Dad walks over with his hand extended.

"It's nice to meet you, son."

"You too, sir," Bennet says, shaking my dad's hand.

"Your name sounds familiar." Dad looks him up and down.

Damon walks over and places his hand on Bennet's shoulder. "Bennet and I went to college together."

Dad points at Bennet. "That's it. You're the boy that got Damon so drunk, he missed his finals."

We all laugh.

"To be fair, that was all Damon. He's the one that bought that cheap vodka," Bennet says, elbowing Damon in the ribs. "Nice to know you blamed me though," he adds on.

Damon shrugs and moves away while rubbing his side. "Hey, I couldn't tell them it was all my fault. I had to miss half of Christmas break to make up my exams. Mom was pissed."

We all laugh before the guys move into the dining room. Mom, Jazz, and myself hang in the kitchen to finish plating the food.

"Man, you guys went all out," I say, adding eggs, French toast, bacon, and sausage to the plate.

"I was hungry. Don't judge me," Jazz says, picking up two plates to take to the dining room.

I laugh. "I'm the last person that will judge you on food," I laugh out. "I'll start some coffee."

I brew the coffee while Mom and Jazz take the plates to the dining room. I take down a tray and fill it with coffee cups and then add the pot of coffee when it's done brewing. Finally, I join the rest of them in the room.

We all talk amongst ourselves while we each pour a cup coffee and take our seats. Mom and Dad sit across from Bennet and myself, and Jazz and Damon are at either end of the table. Finally, we all have our breakfast and coffee.

"So, what's going on?" Dad asks, probably already too coffeed-up to sit still without knowing the reason behind this breakfast date.

"Well, Dad," Damon starts. "We have some good news." He looks at Jazz. "You want to tell them?" He gives her a smile that makes me smile too. I haven't seen him this happy in a long time.

She grins and nods excitedly. "We had a doctor's appointment first thing this morning, and even though it's a little too soon to be able to say one-hundred percent, the doctor had eyes on the baby's sex."

Mom cheers and claps her hands like a child that's too excited to contain herself.

"We're having a…" Jazz starts. "Boy!"

Dad and Damon jump from their seats and hug one another. Their cheers are the loudest of all.

Jazz and Mom hug and I quickly stand and join in.

"Congrats, Jazz," I say as I pull away and take my seat next to Bennet.

I watch as Dad starts to pass all his parenting wisdom down to Damon, and Mom does the same with Jazz. I lean closer to Bennet.

"I guess this is pretty nice, huh?"

He nods and places his arm over my shoulders. "Yeah, they all seem pretty happy."

I can't force my smile to leave my face. I'm just so happy for all of us. I'm happy that Bennet and I get a second chance. I'm happy that my best friend and my brother finally found the love they both knew was there all along. I'm happy that their first son is on his way. And I'm happy for my parents who have been waiting patiently for years for the moment when they become grandparents.

"Maybe we'll think about kids down the road?" I ask lowly, so only Bennet can hear.

He grins and nods. "I'd love to have children with you, Mads." He leans closer and presses a soft kiss to my lips.

We all enjoy breakfast and two pots of coffee before we clean up, and everyone starts to leave. Mom gives me a hug and presses a kiss to my head. "I'm so happy things are finally coming together for you."

"Thanks, Mom," I say around a smile as I watch Bennet and my dad talk and laugh.

Bennet walks my dad to the door, and he quickly kisses my head. "You behave yourself, baby girl. I like this one." He points at Bennet.

"Bye," we all yell as they close the door behind them.

I spin around and wrap my arms around Bennet's waist. Looking up at him, I ask, "What did you and my dad talk so much about?"

He laughs.

"What?"

"He wanted to know when we plan on getting married. He gave Damon and Jazz the house, and he's worried he won't have anything to give you."

I feel my face scrunch. Not because he doesn't have anything to give me. I'm not expecting anything, but I had no idea he gave Damon the house.

I spin around and look at them. They clearly overheard, but they're trying to pretend they have no idea what's going on. Damon is looking at the ceiling, and Jazz is looking at the floor while rubbing her belly.

"Seriously, you two?"

They both jump, trying to explain.

"You can't hit me! I'm pregnant!" Jazz yells, causing us all to laugh.

"When have I ever hit you?" I ask, tilting my head to the side.

She shrugs. "You never know. You are a boxer now."

I snort and roll my eyes.

"I'm sorry, Mads. I didn't think you'd want the house," Damon says.

I laugh. "I don't want the house. Plus, Bennet is building us a new one." I hug him closer and stick my tongue out at them.

They freeze for a second, then realize that I'm not mad about Dad giving them the house. Damon relaxes and turns toward Bennet. "Is that why you bought such a big lot?"

He nods as his hands rub up and down my back. "I was just thinking ahead."

"That's not too far from us. When you guys have kids, they'll get to grow up together," Jazz says.

Bennet and I pull apart, going in separate directions.

"I'm going to finish up in the dining room," Bennet says, taking off.

"I'm going to load the dishwasher," I say, nearly pushing Jazz and Damon out of the way.

Jazz laughs. "I didn't mean now. I just meant, one day."

"We'll see," I tell her with a grin.

———

"Are you sure this looks okay?" I ask, standing back and looking myself over in the mirror.

Bennet adjusts his tie. "You look beautiful," he whispers in my ear just before he presses a kiss to my cheek.

I let out a deep breath. "I'm so nervous. I mean, I know I met your mom before, but she wasn't too happy about us."

Bennet sits on the edge of the bed and pulls on his shoes. "Since my dad has passed, she's a lot different."

"What do you mean?" I ask, applying a light pink lipstick to my lips.

He looks up, and our eyes meet in the mirror. "Before, she was more worried about money and appearances. But now, I think losing my dad has taught her what's really important. She no longer spends her days shopping and taking lavish vacations. She actually sold the house that she and dad shared. She moved into a nice little townhouse just outside the city. She knows she doesn't need that big place just for her. She's downsized quite a bit. She's more focused on family, staying healthy, and spending her time with people she enjoys." He laughs. "She actually joined a book club and a gardening club. She's... I don't know, the happiest I've ever seen her."

I smile as I turn around to face him directly. "That's great. What about your sister?"

He shrugs. "I mean, we won't have any problems out of her. She's one that supports all love. She's very free-spirited. But I'm hoping to talk her into joining the company tonight."

"Does she not want to?"

He stands and walks up to me, wrapping me up in his strong arms. "She wants to make a living off her art, but as we all know, that's hard to do, especially living directly in the city. It's too expensive for what she's making. I'm hoping she comes on, even if it's just part-time to give her some extra cash and insurance. God forbid she gets hurt or sick. I'll be paying her medical bills out of pocket." He leans down and kisses me gently. "Come on. Let's go have dinner." He releases me but keeps my hand in his so he can lead me from the room.

———

BENNET LEADS me into a fancy restaurant and directly to a table that has two women already seated. They both stand and give him a quick hug, then turn to face me.

Bennet's mom smiles as she holds out her hand to shake. "It's wonderful seeing you again, Madeline."

I smile and shake her hand. "You too, Mrs. Windsor." I then turn to his sister.

She leans in and gives me a quick hug. "It's good to finally have a name to put that face to." She pulls away but keeps me at arm's length. "I hope I didn't screw anything up the night you came to the house."

I laugh. "I'm afraid I did that all on my own."

Bennet laughs and rubs my shoulders before pulling out my chair. I sit, and when he slides me forward, he bends down and whispers in my ear, "The only thing you're going to be screwing is me."

His words make my face heat up, and there's no doubt my cheeks are bright red.

He takes his seat between his sister and me. "So, how's everyone doing?"

"I'm doing wonderful. I just got acknowledgment for my beautiful rose garden. I was mentioned in the Tribune," his mom smiles.

"That's great, Mom. What about you, Val?"

She shrugs. "I may be moving in with Mom soon."

Bennet scoffs. "Just come and work at the company and quit being so damn hardheaded."

"What would I be doing?" she asks, eyes cast down at the glass of wine she's swirling around.

"Callan needs an assistant. He's gone through several already this month. None seem to stick."

She rolls her eyes. "That's probably because he's a dumbass." She shakes her head. "I still can't believe Dad let you hire all your buddies."

He laughs. "Well, they're getting the job done, aren't they?"

She shrugs. "I'll think about it."

"What is that you do in the company, Madeline?" Val asks, taking the attention off of her.

"Please, call me Maddie. And I no longer work there. I recently got into data configuration at Chance Security." I pick up my glass and take a drink, hoping this answer doesn't make Bennet start in about me coming back to the company.

"Speaking of that," he says, looking at me.

I roll my eyes, telling him now isn't the time.

"What do you say we order, huh?" he changes the subject.

We all pick up our menus, and the conversation drifts off to easier topics.

I knew, at some point, Bennet would mention me coming back to the company, and I've been dreading talking about it. It's not that I hated working there. In fact, when nobody knew about us, it was fun being able to sneak into his office and have a little dirty time. But now that everyone knows, I don't know if I can ever show my face there again. Especially in that office, or on that floor entirely. Plus, I'm really liking my new job. It has good hours, great benefits, and the pay is more than I've ever made before.

The topic isn't brought up again through the rest of dinner, but the moment Bennet and I slide into the car, he asks again.

"What are your plans for working, Maddie? Are you going to stay where you're at? Do you ever see yourself coming back? Or do you not want to work at all?"

My eyes cut in his direction. "Of course I want to work."

He flinches from my harsh tone. "Okay, I'm just letting you know that you don't have to if you don't want to."

"What would I do? Sit around and drink tea all day?" I ask sarcastically.

He snorts. "God, I'd hope not. But I miss you at the office." He reaches over and takes my hand in his, his thumb gently rubbing the back and forth.

"I can't show my face there, Bennet. I mean, the moment I walk into that building, I will feel like everyone is talking about me."

"Who cares?" he asks.

I turn and look at him. "I do. You don't know what it's like having everyone say you got something you worked hard for just from being with one person."

He laughs. "Do you know who you're talking to? I've had a million people talk badly about me because of who my father is. I've been told

I never would've made it on my own, that I owe everything to my father. You know what I did?" he asks, glancing at me.

I shrug.

"I proved them all wrong. I took Dad's company and pushed it into becoming one of the top business in Chicago. I admit, Dad started it off right, but if it weren't for me, it wouldn't be worth nearly as much as it is now. And all those people that said I couldn't do it, they all shut the fuck up. And now when I see them, they smile and suck up, acting polite. And I just rub it in their smug faces. You can do the same."

I smile, wanting to laugh, but I hold it back. "I just want you. Not that job." I shake my head while looking at him.

He slows the car to a stop in the middle of a traffic jam and leans toward me. "If that's what you want, Maddie." He kisses me softly. "I just want you happy."

I smile. "Thank you."

He sits back in his seat, and my mind begins to drift. He just wants me happy.

Well, I want him happy too. And if working there would make him happy, shouldn't I do it? I know he would do it for me. Should I quit my job and come back to work for my boyfriend? Would I be happy doing that?

I let out a deep breath, confused and completely unsure.

22

BENNET

"If I asked you to quit your job, would you?" she asks out of nowhere.

I look over at her in the passenger seat. "What?"

"If I asked you to resign or sell or quit, would you?" Her face is serious, eyes narrowed on me.

I turn to look back out the windshield, thinking it over. "I guess I would have to ask why."

"To make me happy. If I said it's me or that company, which would you choose?"

"You, without question," I state.

I'm not sure if that's the answer she wanted or not. She turns to look forward once again.

"Where's this coming from?"

"You said you just wanted me happy?"

"I did."

"Well, I want you happy too. And if coming back to work there would make you happy, shouldn't I be more than willing to give you that?"

Now I see where this is going. "Mads, I didn't mean anything by it. I'm happy just having you in my life. I'm happy being able to touch you and kiss you and share our lives together. That's all I meant."

She nods. "I know. But me working there would make you happy," she states.

"I guess it would. It wouldn't make me unhappy."

"Okay. You're willing to do anything I ask. I'll do it. I want you to know that I'd do anything you ask too. I want our relationship to be a team. I don't want always to get what I want while you never get what you want. I want us to be equals. I have your back, and you have mine."

I laugh softly as I press a kiss to the back of her hand, squeezing it gently. "I'll get you your own office. Hell, you can have my office if you want it."

She looks over at me and smiles. "Thank you, but my own office will do just fine." Her eyes flash over to me. "Oh, and I want more pay. You have to at least match my salary at Chance."

"Deal. New office. Salary matched. What else?"

She places her finger on her chin as she thinks it over. "Ummm, I want paid vacation time, unlimited access to your office any time I want to visit, and a 401K."

I laugh. "You drive a hard bargain, but I accept."

I pull into the parking lot and shut off the car. "Now, the big questions: where are we going to live?"

She smiles and steps out of the car, leaving me to chase after her. I smack her on the ass playfully as I pass, opening the door to the building for her. When we step into the elevator, I spin her around and press her back to the wall with my lips to against hers. Her hands come up and thread through my hair that's beginning to grow out. She gently pulls it, breaking our kiss.

"I don't care where we live, as long as we're together."

I grin from hearing her words, moving my lips back to hers. My hands have a mind of their own, traveling her body, massaging and caressing. My dick hardens, and I grind it against her core. She lets out a breathy moan of excitement.

I move my hands up to her cheeks, pushing her hair away from her face. "You're so beautiful," I whisper. "I don't want to wait to see where the future takes us. Let's create our future." I place her on her feet and drop down to one knee.

Her eyes grow wide and her lips part. I reach into my jacket pocket and pull out a small box.

"How long have you had that?" she asks.

"My mother gave it to me tonight at dinner. It was my great-grandmother's ring. It's been passed down for generations." I open the box, and the light in the elevator catches the diamond perfectly.

"Madeline Michelle Strickland, I've loved you since the moment my eyes met yours. I don't want to walk another day on this earth without being able to say you're mine. Will you please marry me?"

Her gaping mouth turns into a smile as she nods slowly. "Yes," she whispers.

I take the ring from the box with shaking hands and slide it onto her finger. The instant she pulls her hand back to examine the ring, I stand and pick her up against me, kissing her with everything I have.

I don't know how long the door to the elevator has been open, but I turn and walk us through it, down the hallway, and to her apartment. I manage to get the door open with one hand, and I carry her through, kicking it closed behind me. I set her on the island in the kitchen, and immediately she starts pushing my jacket over my shoulders.

I shrug out of it quickly, letting it fall to the floor at my feet. My hands land on her thighs, working her dress up her legs. When I get it high enough, I'm surprised to find her completely bare underneath. Her hands are unfastening my belt and pants, and before I know it, she's working my length up and down in her hand.

I grab her hips and pull her to the edge of the counter before positioning myself at her entrance. I thrust into her, and the moment we become one, we both let out a relieved moan, finally back to the way we're meant to be.

My lips move from her mouth, down to her neck, and I'm in such a rush to taste her, my hands begin pulling at her dress. The fabric tears and the sound of tiny beads peppering the tile fills my ears. I pause and look around. She laughs but pulls my mouth back to hers.

Finally, I take her in my arms and carry her through the apartment, never separating, until I can lay her down in bed where I can move between her beautiful thighs all night long.

When I place her on the bed, she rolls over, getting up on her knees as she glances over her shoulder at me. I bite my lower lip, getting even more excited. With my hands on her hips, I pull her toward the edge of the bed until I can slide back inside her. In this position, she feels tighter, and it makes all my muscles constrict to hold back the orgasm that's begging to be set free. As I rock my hips back and forth, she moves into my thrusts, making me feel like I'm deeper inside her than I've ever been. Her muscles begin to twitch around me, and I let my hand move around her hips and down to her clit. The extra stimulation has her crying out my name over and over until I feel her relax. I remove myself from her, and with one hand, gently push her hips to the side where she rolls over onto her back. As I begin climbing up the bed, she places a hand on my chest and urges me back. At this point, I'm so wound-up that I can't fight her. I'll give it to her any way I can. She straddles me and slides me back inside her. I latch onto her hips, pulling her down harder each time she begins to slide me out of her.

I can tell she's about to come again, and I'm about to lose all sense of control. At the last second, I roll us over and drive into her so deep she lets out a scream. Her nails dig into my back, and teeth bite down on my shoulder. She's so hot and tight around me; I have no choice but to let my release go at the same time she lets out a soft whimper.

"I love you, Maddie," I whisper into her hair as we both stop to catch our breath and regain control over our bodies.

———

MONDAY MORNING ROLLS AROUND, and Maddie is a nervous wreck as we ride my private elevator up to my office together. "Don't be so worried. We're going to make sure everyone in the building knows that you are soon to be part-owner of Windsor Wealth Management."

"What? How?" she asks, icy eyes popping up to meet mine.

"We're throwing an engagement party in the conference room. Food, drinks, and cake for everyone. Come on; we're running late." I take her hand and pull her from the elevator, down the hall, and into the conference room.

We walk in, and everyone yells, "Congratulations!" Then all their eyes narrow on Maddie standing next to me. Their mouths drop open as they force themselves to recover quickly.

"Thank you for leaving your desks for a moment to celebrate with us," I tell them. "Please, everyone, help yourselves to the food and drinks."

Maddie is standing by my side, quiet and worried. Her eyes are dashing around the room, and they're filled with fear.

"Madeline and I are aware of the rumors going around the building," I start addressing the group of employees that are gathered around. "And I am here to clear up anything you may have questions about. I didn't meet Madeline until Brian, our usual data guy, was out sick. She was hired for his position but ended up being put in the mailroom on hold. When she was called to action, she went above and beyond what any other person in her position could have done. Which is why she landed the job full-time. We started working together, became friends, and it was undeniable the feelings I was having for her. We had been together for weeks before any of you found out. I assure you, this won't affect any aspect of your jobs or normal working day. Madeline and I know how to be professional around the workplace. But just so you all know, when we're married, Madeline will be part-owner of this company. So, I suggest you all treat her with respect moving forward."

Everyone starts talking at once, saying congratulations and best wishes. They go back to their small groups and the conversations they were having before we even walked into the room. I take Maddie's hand and pull her into my office; the second the door is shut between us, I move my mouth to hers. She lets out a deep, content breath against my lips.

"God, I thought I was going to explode if I didn't get to taste you soon," I whisper, allowing my hands to roam her beautiful body.

She giggles. "What happened to being professional, Mr. Windsor?" she teases.

"Fuck being professional," I whisper as I walk her toward my desk.

———

"WHERE ARE WE GOING?" Maddie asks as I lead her from the office into my car.

"We have some things to go over." I climb behind the wheel and pull out of the garage.

"What kind of things?" she asks, turning her upper body to face me.

"Well, first off, if we're going to be living outside the city at times, you're going to need a vehicle."

Her eyes stretch wide. "I can't afford a new car," she points out.

"It's on me, Maddie."

"What? No, Bennet. I don't want your money," she argues, crossing her arms over her chest.

"Whether you want it or not is not up to you. We're getting married. Half of everything is already yours. I don't want to have my money and you to have your money. I want us both to have our money. Understand? Teamwork, remember?" I flash her a quick smile and shoot her a wink from quoting her words.

She laughs. "Fine. But I'm not getting something this fancy." She motions toward my Mercedes.

"You can get whatever you want," I assure her.

"Even a Lambo?" I can tell she's teasing me by the way she's holding back a smile.

I laugh. "If you wish."

She shakes her head and rolls her eyes, but she doesn't argue.

We get out at the car lot, and we walk around several times. But every time she checks out one car, I notice her always looking back at another. I know the only reason she hasn't spoken on it yet is the price tag.

I look over at her. "Just get the one you want. It doesn't matter how much it cost."

"But I said I didn't want a Mercedes, and now I'm totally in love with that G-Wagon," she pouts.

I laugh, wrap my arm around her shoulders, and lead her to the blacked-out G-Wagon. I open the door and motion for her to climb inside.

She sits behind the wheel, and I see her face and eyes light up. "Is this the one?" I ask.

She smiles wide and nods.

"Let's go do the paperwork."

Once everything is signed and done, I have the G-Wagon delivered to the house and we go to our next assignment. I hit the highway and drive out of the city. Her hand is in mine as the music softly plays over the speakers. The top is down, and the sun is shining. Every time I look at her, her skin is glowing while her dark hair flies about crazily. Just looking at her makes me smile. Being able to reach out and hold her hand brightens my day. I know one thing for sure: I'm going to thank God every day for bringing her into my life. I will cherish every day I get to spend with her and call her mine. It almost seems impossible that I'm this happy, and a part of me doesn't want to trust it. But that's old me speaking. Maddie has taught me so much about love and trust and happiness. I think it's about time that I start to trust us. Not her or me, but us together as a team.

I exit the highway and make a few turns on some side streets. We drive through a small town that has nothing but a gas station, a home-style restaurant, and a couple independent business, and finally, we're home—or our soon to be home.

"Is this your shop?" she asks, unbuckling and stepping out of the car.

"Yep. Follow me." I take her hand and lead her to the backside of the property where there's a big pond. I turn us around and point at the place the house is going. "The house is going to be over there. The plans have a back porch so we can sit out there at sunset and watch the sun leave the sky over the pond. There's going to be four bedrooms upstairs with three baths. Then downstairs there's the kitchen, living room, dining room, bathroom, laundry room, and office. What do you think?"

She turns to face me and wraps her arms around my neck. "I think it'll be perfect." She closes the distance between us, pressing her lips to mine.

"Want to see the garage?" I ask, pulling her back up the property and to the pole barn. I unlock the door and turn off the alarm. The garage isn't much, just a typical garage, but the tools and car parts are everywhere, with a half-finished car parked in the center. I tap it on the front fender. "This will be the first one to roll out. What do you think?"

She smiles as she walks closer. "I think we need to welcome it to the family, don't you?" she says, walking closer.

"What did you have in mind?"

On her walk over to me, she's slowly working her sundress up her thighs, then her flat, toned stomach, past her full chest, and over her head. She tosses it my way, and it lands on the top of the car.

She's finally within arm's reach, and I grab her, picking her up and setting her on the hood. My mouth moves to hers, and her hands get busy freeing me from my jeans. I lay her back as I position myself at her opening. One hand guides myself into her while the other travels her body.

"I love you, Bennet," she whispers while I take from my body to give to hers.

"I love you too, Maddie," I say, thrusting into her, filling her until she cries out.

When we've both lost ourselves, I pull her up, and we both fix our clothing. She looks at the car with a smile. "That's better, right?"

I look down at the hood of the car and see her ass print. I laugh. "Much better."

As we walk out of the garage and I turn to lock the door, my eyes land on the car, and a smile spreads across my face. "I may have a hard time selling that car now." She laughs but takes my hand and pulls me back to the driveway where we parked.

"You know, I think this property would make for a beautiful wedding."

I look over at her. "I think you're right."

"How much time do we have until the house is done?"

I shrug. "Depends on when we start it."

"Can it be done by next spring?"

I start the car. "I think so. I'll call the construction company in the morning and give them the go-ahead to start."

She leans over the center console. "Thank you," she whispers, pressing her lips to mine.

"Anything, Maddie," I whisper against them. "Always."

23

MADDIE

MONTHS LATER...

THE PHONE RINGING wakes me from a dead sleep. "Hello?" I ask, rubbing my eyes as I look at the clock to see that it's only two in the morning.

"Maddie, it's happening!" Jazz says, pain evident in her voice.

"On my way!" I hang up and throw the blankets back, shaking Bennet.

"Wake up! Jazz is in labor!"

He springs from the bed. "Okay, I'm up. I'm up," he mumbles, rubbing his eyes.

I run to the walk-in closet and dig around for some clothes. I'm changed in less than a minute. I'm sitting on the bed, pulling on my shoes when Bennet walks in the room with his toothbrush hanging out of his mouth.

"What are you doing? We have to hurry. I don't want to miss it."

"Okay, okay," he mumbles around his toothbrush. "Doesn't it take like hours to have a baby?"

I shrug. "How am I supposed to know? I've never had a baby before."

He waves his hand in the air. "I think we'll have plenty of time."

We get to the hospital almost an hour later, and Jazz is already in the delivery room. I stand in the waiting room, arms crossed and tapping my foot. "I told you we needed to hurry."

He scrunches down into his chair. "Okay, I'm sorry, but we didn't miss it," he says, looking over at my mom and dad who are almost asleep from being drug out of bed at this ungodly hour.

It feels like hours pass, but Damon comes running into the waiting room. "He's here!" he yells, causing everyone to jump awake.

Bennet jumps up and shakes his hand. "Congrats, man."

"When can I see them?" I ask.

"They're getting them cleaned up now, and as soon as we move into a normal room, I'll come get you guys," he says, hugging everyone before rushing back to be with Jazz and his newborn son.

Finally, I feel like I can relax, knowing that everyone is safe and sound. I collapse into the empty chair at Bennet's side, and he wraps his arms around my shoulders.

"Would it be crazy to think about doing this again, but this time, having it be us in there?" he whispers quietly so as to not disturb my parents, who are slipping in and out of consciousness.

I shrug one shoulder. "I haven't given it much thought yet," I lie. Here lately, I've been thinking about it a lot. Every time Jazz would complain about having some weird pregnancy symptom, whenever we'd go shopping for more baby clothes, every time a baby passes by me, I'm thinking about it. And while I think it would be great to have a child someday, I'm still not sure that I want to give all of my time to another human being.

"Would I sound selfish if I say that I just want to spend a little more time, just you and me?"

He rests his forehead against mine. "It can be just us until the day we die, Maddie." Gently, he presses his lips to mine.

"Oh, I know. I think we're getting caught up in this whole baby business. Instead of saying things we could do with a baby, let's say things that we can do without one. Like, instead of having a baby, we could jet-set across the world at the drop of a hat."

He smiles. "We could climb Mt. Everest."

"We could skinny dip in the ocean while getting drunk."

He laughs. "We could spend the rest of our lives holding one another while we sleep instead of arguing over who's going to feed the baby."

"We could kiss instead of changing diapers," I add on.

"We could…" he starts, but Damon walks back into the room.

"Are you guys ready to meet him?"

We all jump up like we've been lit on fire.

Damon still hasn't lost the smile. "This way," he says, leading us down the hall.

We all walk into Jazz's room, and she's laying in bed, holding what looks like a balled-up blanket. As we draw closer, I see just the touch of pink skin.

I go to the side of the bed and lean over. Somehow, I forget to breathe. My eyes fill with tears. "Oh, my goodness. Can I hold him?" I ask.

She smiles. "Of course."

Damon takes him from Jazz and places him in my arms.

"Don't forget to support his head," Jazz says quickly. I look at her and can see the nerves rolling off of her.

"Don't worry." I sit down and turn him so I can look at him directly.

He has pitch-black hair, just like Damon. And his eyes are baby blue, just like Jazz. He has a tiny little nose, the softest, smoothest skin that has just a touch of baby pink, and chubby little cheeks. I lift him against my chest and press the softest of kisses to the top of his head. I inhale his scent deeply. He smells so sweet. I feel my heart grow wings and fly away.

"What's his name?" I ask.

Jazz and Damon look at one another then turn back to the family.

"His name is Gavin Scott Strickland," Damon announces, and the whole room practically cheers—quietly as to not disturb the baby.

"Hi, Gavin. I'm your aunt Maddie," I introduce myself. "One of these days, we're going to be like this." I lift up one hand and show him my crossed fingers. "I'll keep all your secrets and won't tell your mean mommy and daddy." I laugh.

"Okay, time's up. Give me my grandson," Mom says, sitting down beside me and reaching for the baby.

I give him one last kiss and pass him over. I stand to give Dad room to sit down, and I stand with Bennet. He wraps his arm around me. "So, what are you thinking now?"

I shrug one shoulder while I watch everyone fall over baby Gavin. Finally, I look up at him. "I think I'll make a really good aunt."

He smiles. "You will," he agrees.

"But I don't think I want to be a mom, if that's okay with you." I wrap my arms around his neck.

"Then it's you and me against the world, Maddie. All I need in this life is you." Slowly, he leans down and kisses me softly.

―――――

MONTHS PASS, and it feels like no time at all. But the next thing I know, our house is built, and we're leaving the mansion to stay in our country home. The wedding is just around the corner, and now that the house is finished, I can focus solely on that. Everything has already been done and picked out. Now it's just time to choose how to set up.

When I pull into the driveway, Benet pulls in next to me. We both exit our vehicles and meet in the front.

"Come on. I have to carry you over the threshold." He scoops me up against him.

I laugh. "But we're not married yet."

"This is our home. It's mandatory." He walks us across the yard, onto the covered front porch, and opens the screen door. I love everything about this house. It really is picture-perfect, from the bushes and flowers to the raw wood porch, down to the white screen door.

He slides the key into the lock, and the door opens easily. He takes a step in, and before I can even glance around the house, his mouth is on mine.

"I love you so much, Maddie," he whispers against my lips.

"I love you too, Bennet," I reply, pulling his lips back to mine.

I can't wait to start our new lives together. I'm looking forward to the wedding, the honeymoon, and everything else we may do in the next fifty years. But I know one thing without a doubt: our love, it happened fast and hard. It's all-consuming. We couldn't be without the other because it wasn't something that we chose to begin with. It chose us. And with a love as crazy, strong, and passionate as ours, there's no room for anyone else. We're selfish with one another because we can be, because we choose to be. I don't know where life will take us, but I know that I won't ever regret not taking the typical route of raising children. Because in fifty or sixty years, I'll have a life-time of memories to look back on.

"Promise me something?" I ask.

"Anything," he breathes out.

"Promise me that we won't ever grow up. We come first every time."

He smiles wide. "I promise," he agrees, pulling me back in.

————

OUR WEDDING DAY APPROACHES, and even though I'm ready and want to marry him, I'm still nervous. Jazz helps me get into my dress, and as she zips it up, I look myself over in the mirror.

"This all seems so crazy," I tell her.

Her eyes look up and lock on mine in the mirror. "Why? It's a long time coming if you ask me."

I laugh. "In a way, I guess. But I was never one of those girls that planned their perfect wedding day. Hell, until Bennet asked me, I didn't even want to get married."

"So, why'd you say yes?"

"Because it was him and I can't deny him." I laugh.

She giggles and shakes her head. "When are the babies coming?"

She arches an eyebrow.

"What babies?" I ask, and she thinks I'm joking.

"The babies! When are you going to start trying to have kids?" Her eyes are now stretched wide.

I laugh. "Oh, no. I'm not having kids. Are you crazy?"

"Seriously? Who's Gavin supposed to grow up with if you don't have kids?" She's standing up right now, hands on her hips behind me.

I turn around to face her instead of looking through the mirror. "Jazz, you know me. You know I've never in my life wanted children. And Bennet didn't either, even though he's completely happy doing so if I change my mind. But," I shake my head as I sit down to slide on my shoes, "we want a lifetime of each other. We're selfish and don't want to share our lives with anyone else. We want to be able to take a trip at the drop of the hat. I don't want to spend the next fifteen years doing homework or ushering kids to soccer practice. I just want to live my life with my husband."

Jazz smiles. "I think that was the most beautiful selfish thing I've ever heard."

I laugh and stand up. "Come on, let's get me hitched."

We both leave the room and head down the stairs and into the kitchen where I look out the French doors onto the property. Everyone is in their place. The chairs are filled with friends and family on both sides, and Bennet is standing ahead of them all. He looks up, and our eyes lock. I see the corners of his lips turn up.

"Ready to go?" Dad asks, holding out his arm.

"Ready as I'll ever be," I tell him.

The doors open and the music filters in. First Jazz walks out holding her bouquet of white and pink roses. Then Valerie follows after her. Finally, it's my turn. The hold Dad has on me tightens just before he pulls me forward.

On my walk down the aisle, I can't look around at the guests, the flowers, or how beautiful everything looks. All I see is Bennet. To many, he probably looks nervous, but I know that isn't the case. He's not nervous; he's excited—he's itching to have me up there where we can start the first day of the rest of our lives. He's practically bouncing from foot to foot, his hands are clasped together, and I can see the muscles in his hands twitching. But his eyes, they're not dancing around. They're stuck on me.

When Dad and I make it to the altar, the preacher asks, "Who gives this woman away?"

"Her mother and I do," Dad says, pressing a kiss to my cheek before walking away and taking his seat next to my mom.

Bennet finally looks calm and collected as he reaches out and pulls me closer to him, mouthing the words: I love you.

Neither of us were big on the idea of having to write our own vows, so we stick to the normal ones. We both recite the vows the preacher reads off to us, and then we slide on each other's rings.

Finally, the preacher says those magic words: "I now pronounce you husband and wife. You may kiss your bride."

No sooner have the words escaped his lips than I find myself against Bennet's hard chest, his mouth pressed to mine while his hand cups my cheek, holding me to him. The crowd around us cheers loudly. So loud, it almost seems like it's a prerecorded round of applause playing in the background. I tune it out, focusing on my heart that's pounding with excitement, the way his hands are touching me softly, but also holding me to him firmly, and how his soft lips mold to mine.

When he pulls away, we both have smiles on our faces, and instead of us walking down the aisle, he picks me up and carries me down it, back into the house, kicking the door closed behind us. My back hits the wall, and his body is against mine. His hands are a mess, trying to touch all of me at the same time. My fluffy dress is a pile of material as he works it up to my waist. His hand reaches out and touches me. The moment he finds me bare beneath my dress, just like I know he likes me, he's racing to free himself.

"I can't wait another second to be inside my wife." He places himself at my entrance and thrusts into me.

I gasp. "What about our guests?"

"It's just you and me, Maddie. We live our way," he says against my lips as he rolls his hips.

EPILOGUE

BENNET

"This was a great idea," Maddie says as I take my seat next to her on the deck of the yacht we rented.

I laugh and hand over her drink. She sits up and her bikini top that she untied stays on the chair. My eyes zero in on her amazing chest.

She giggles and rolls her eyes as she takes a sip. "Seriously, Mr. Windsor? How many times have we had sex now?"

"It doesn't matter how many times we've been together. I'm always going to enjoy looking at your body." I reach for her, but she pulls away to tease me.

"Oh, no you don't, Mister. You owe me one, remember?" She points her index finger at me.

I think back on last night when we docked to get a little time off the boat. Even though we did a ton of things with our time, all I can think about is how she pulled me into the dark alley, dropped to her knees, and sucked me until I had spilled every last drop.

I smile just from thinking about it. "Alright. You're right." I stand up and sit on her lounge chair. She slouches back, placing one leg on either side of me. Slowly, she unties the strings on her white bikini but leaves the material draped over her center.

I flip myself onto my stomach, lowering my face to her lap. Using my teeth, I pull the material away and glide my tongue between her folds. Her head rolls back, and a hum escapes her lips. Tasting her, it turns me on, and already my dick is begging me to slide into her. But I owe her one. I force myself to give her what she needs before demanding more.

I flick my tongue against her clit, back and forth until her knees are shaking and her muscles are tightened with anticipation. When I slide two fingers into her, her release breaks. Her hands latch onto the edges of the chair as her hips rise off the seat. She has gasps and moans escaping her beautiful lips. She calls my name over and over. When her release ends, her legs are still shaking. But I steady them as I pull my shorts down and slide between her parted knees. As I kiss her deeply, I position myself at her opening and rock my hips forward, thrusting into her with as much force as I can. Her back arches as she moans into my mouth. My hands find her hips, holding firm as I rock into her, pushing us both to our limits. After she's come down from her high, I let mine go.

Being with her, it's something like I've never felt before. Not only on the love aspect of it, but physically. I've never been turned on like this with anyone else. My body has never physically caved the touch of a certain person before. But now, I'm a goner. I've been a goner since the first time I was allowed to touch her. And I'm never going back. She owns every part of me: body, heart, and soul.

As my hips slow, I rest my head on her chest and listen to the way her heart pounds for me. It's like a song that's just for me, a song that it takes the two of us to make. If I die tomorrow, I'll die a happy man because she loved me. Before we met, I didn't know the point of life. It all seemed so meaningless to me. But then I found her, and she gave everything meaning.

"When is our flight home?" she asks from beneath me.

"In a couple hours." I lift my head to look into her eyes. "Are you happy to be going back home?"

She shrugs. "Not really, but I do miss my family. We've been sailing across the world for three months now."

I nod as I lift myself off of her. "It's a good thing I gave Damon that promotion. I'm not sure the company would've gone this long without me." When we planned this little adventure, it was set for two weeks, tops. Here we are three months into it, and neither of us are ready to go home yet. We've seen things some people can only dream of. We've drunk homemade wine with locals, we slept under the stars, had sex beneath a waterfall, danced in a rainstorm in the middle of town with people crowding around to watch. My life and heart are full, and all because I met her when I least expected it.

———

"HAPPY BIRTHDAY, GAVIN," Maddie says, rushing into the house she grew up in. He comes crawling toward her, and she bends down, picking him up and hugging him close.

"How's it feel to be one year old today?" she asks, even though she knows she's not getting an answer.

"Hey!" Jazz says, walking around the corner. "Welcome back." She gives us both a quick hug. "That trip must have been pretty good to stay for three whole months."

We both laugh. "We just weren't ready to leave our little paradise," she says, looking at Gavin.

"I don't blame you one bit. If I had the chance to drop life and travel the world, I damn sure would."

"Why don't you?" she asks, bouncing Gavin up and down gently.

Jazz places her hand on her hip. "I have too much responsibility. I have this little guy, we both have work, a house, bills to pay. Not to mention, this little bundle of joy on the way." She points at her stomach.

Maddie's eyes grow wide. "You're pregnant?"

Jazz smiles and nods. "Fingers crossed for a little girl!"

Maddie and Jazz both squeal and hug, nearly smashing Gavin between them.

I reach over and take the poor kid. "Come on, little man. Let's go find Daddy and get away from these crazy women."

I walk through the house, bouncing Gavin and looking for Damon. I catch sight of him outside on the back patio. He's standing over the grill with an apron on and a beer in his hand. His dad is sitting at the table, looking like he's talking a mile a minute.

I laugh and shake my head. "Looks like grandpa is getting a little buzzed, Gavin," I mumble, opening the door and stepping out.

"There's my brother-in-law I haven't seen in months," Damon says, spinning around. "Can you believe he just handed over his company and took off, jet-setting around the world?" he says to his dad.

I laugh. "I didn't hand over shit. That company is still mine, and I'm taking it back." I hand him over his son. "I heard the good news, Daddy," I say, shaking his hand.

He smiles wide and nods his head. "Yeah, Gavin is going to have a baby brother or sister."

"That's awesome, man. Congrats."

"There's beer in that cooler," Damon says, placing Gavin in his outdoor play pin and pointing toward the house where a red cooler sets.

I walk over, grab a beer, and come back to sit at the table. "So, what's been going on?"

He shakes his head. "Nothing new. What about you? Do anything fun on that vacation?"

"Besides your sister?" I say, giving him hell.

"Hey now," he says, pointing his spatula at me. "You're not on vacation anymore, Juicy."

I hold up my hands, palms facing him to let him know I'm throwing in the towel.

Jazz and Maddie come walking out. Maddie grabs a beer and comes to sit on my lap while Jazz picks up the baby and sits down beside us.

"Tell me about the vacation. Where'd you go? What'd you do?" she says, bouncing Gavin up and down on her legs.

"We went everywhere. We rented a yacht and just sailed around the ocean. We'd dock from time to time to go sight-seeing and gather more supplies. We stayed up late, slept all day, had sex anytime we wanted," Maddie says.

"Hey, I'm right here," Damon says, looking over at the horrified look on her dad's face as well.

Maddie waves him off but gives her dad a sheepish grin. "It was amazing just to be able to drop everything and go wherever we wanted, when we wanted. I'm glad to be home, though. We missed you guys."

Jazz looks up at Damon. "We should do that. Take a vacation before I'm too pregnant to do anything."

Damon nods his head. "Okay, sounds good to me. Where do you want to go?"

"Hey, why don't you talk Mom and Dad into keeping Gavin and we'll all go out on the yacht for a couple of weeks."

Everyone laughs.

"Last time you said a couple of weeks, you were gone for three months, Maddie," Jazz says. "I can't be away from Gavin that long. Can I?" she asks, holding him up and kissing his cheek.

Maddie rolls her eyes. "I wouldn't do that if you guys were with us. It'll be fun. We can lounge around and get a tan; we can find some cool shops and beaches, get drunk every night… Well, you can't, but I can." She laughs.

Jazz hugs the baby. "I'll think about it."

Maddie leans closer and whispers in my ear. "Come with me." She stands up and walks into the house.

I set my beer down and stand up; everyone looks at me. "Um, I'll be right back. Maddie wants to show me something."

None of them say anything as I walk into the house to find Maddie waiting in the kitchen.

"What's up?"

"I want to show you my childhood bedroom. Come on." She grabs my hand and pulls me up the stairs and into a small, freshly painted yellow room.

She scrunches up her nose. "It used to be pink. And my bed was right here." She motions with her arms.

I nod. "Cool."

She laughs. "You're not getting it, are you?"

"Getting what?" I ask, confused.

"I want to have sex." She flashes me a wide smile.

"Right now?" I ask, pointing at the floor.

She nods. "I never had sex in this room. The first time should be with you—before they fill it up with another baby." She reaches over and grabs my belt, pulling me closer.

I laugh. "I fuckin' love you," I say, wrapping my arms around her and pulling her against me as I lower us both to the floor.

———

"HEY, YOUR SISTER IS HERE," Jazz says the moment we walk down the stairs. "She's out back." She picks up the birthday cake and leads us out.

Everyone starts singing happy birthday, and I come to a stop next to Val. "What's going on?"

"I'll take it," she admits.

"You'll take what?" I ask, crossing my arms over my chest and watching everyone gather around Gavin.

"The job. I'll take the job. Okay?" She crosses her arms over her chest, and her face is a little puckered.

My head jerks in her direction. "You'll take the job?"

She nods. "At this point, I have to. I lost my apartment and had to move back in with Mom. All my credit cards are maxed out. I'm finally selling out." She hangs her head, defeated.

I bump her shoulder with mine. "You're not selling out. You're being strong and doing what you have to do to survive. There's nothing wrong with that."

She looks up, and her bloodshot eyes meet mine. The corners of her mouth turn up slightly. "I didn't think of it like that."

I wrap my arm around her shoulders and pull her to my side. "See there; things are looking up already."

"Val, come get a piece of cake," Maddie says.

I release her as she joins the rest of the family.

Standing back alone, looking over this amazing family I now have, I feel my heart inside my chest nearly double. My life used to consist of just me, working and going to the gym—sleeping with whatever random woman I could find. And at the time, I thought I had it all. But now, I see how much I was missing. I have a woman that loves me wholeheartedly—so much so, she doesn't want to share our time with anyone else. I have a great job and a wonderful family. I have people close to me now, people to share my life with. It's funny how looking back, you can see all the little things that got you to where you are now. But back then, looking forward, none of it made sense. I thank God every day that Maddie was the one that got under my skin. I'm thankful for every look, every touch, every time she whispers, "I love you." I'm thankful that we get to spend every day together, that we can do whatever we want, whenever we want. I love that she's wild and free, but my favorite part is that she is her own person. She doesn't bend to what society says she should be.

She looks up and waves me over with a smile. Her icy eyes are lit up, and her ivory skin is glowing from our lovemaking. Her lips are a little swollen from our kisses. Just seeing her happy like this, it makes my heart double its pace. She steals the air from my lungs and makes my muscles tighten. I walk over and place my hand on the small of her back, pulling her in for a kiss. She presses her lips to mine and looks into my eyes.

"Isn't this perfect?" she asks quietly. "All of us together, happy and growing."

I smile and nod.

Now, I know that I have it all.

CHECK OUT THE REST OF THE SERIES HERE

Make Her Mine Series

My Best Friend's Brother
My Boss's Sister
My Best Friend's Ex
The Friend Agreement (Coming this March)

ALSO BY ALEXIS WINTER

Hate That I Love You: Castille Hotel Series Prequel

Want this prequel for FREE? Sign up here to get it along with a second free novel delivered right to your inbox!

Castille Hotel Series

Business & Pleasure: Castille Hotel Series Book 1

Baby Mistake: Castille Hotel Series Book 2

Fake It: Castille Hotel Series Book 3

South Side Boys Series

Damaged-Book 1

Broken-Book 2

Wrecked-Book 3 (Coming December)

Redemption-Book 4 (Coming February)

Mountain Ridge Series

Just Friends: Mountain Ridge Book 1

Protect Me: Mountain Ridge Book 2

Baby Shock: Mountain Ridge Book 3

Claimed by Him: A Contemporary Romance 6 Book Collection

ALL BOOKS CAN BE READ AS STAND-ALONE READS WITHIN THESE SERIES

ABOUT THE AUTHOR

Alexis Winter is a contemporary romance author who loves to share her steamy stories with the world. She specializes in billionaires, alpha males and the women they love.

If you love to curl up with a good romance book you will certainly enjoy her work. Whether it's a story about an innocent young woman learning about the world or a sassy and fierce heroin who knows what she wants you,'re sure to enjoy the happily ever afters she provides.

When Alexis isn't writing away furiously, you can find her exploring the Rocky Mountains, traveling, enjoying a glass of wine or petting a cat.

You can find her books on Amazon or at
https://www.alexiswinterauthor.com/

Follow Alexis Winter below for access to advanced copies of upcoming releases, fun giveaways and exclusive deals!

Printed by Amazon Italia Logistica S.r.l.
Torrazza Piemonte (TO), Italy

12953018R00121